About the author

Kathryn is a single mum of two boys, originally from Sheffield, South Yorkshire, but now lives in a small town in Lancashire. As well as writing, Kathryn loves everything creative, especially cross stitching; she owns a small arts and crafts business which she runs from the local indoor market. She loves to watch sports, including Formula One and football, which her eldest son plays. She also loves to travel and explore cultural places; she lived in Greece for five years and also worked in the US for a summer season. Kathryn recently graduated from the Open University, completing her degree in Humanities.

CROSSING LINES

KATHRYN PANA

CROSSING LINES

Vanguard Press

A CIP catalogue record for this title is
available from the British Library.

ISBN 978 1 78465 797 0

*Vanguard Press is an imprint of
Pegasus Elliot MacKenzie Publishers Ltd.*
www.pegasuspublishers.com

First Published in 2020

**Vanguard Press
Sheraton House Castle Park
Cambridge England**

Printed & Bound in Great Britain

Dedication

For my boys who are my everything.
For Karen for your friendship, support and
encouragement.
For the staff at Colne Library for the amazing job
you do and the kindness that you always show.

Prologue

Two months earlier

Kathy Hill sat on her sofa. She looked at the street below. She had moved to this street three years ago and she realised each person that walked past, she had no idea who they were; she had never even had a conversation with any of them. The only person she knew was the lady who rented the apartment below her home, a house that she had inherited from her grandmother. It had been a sad time when her grandmother had passed on, as she was the only person in her family who could see Kathy for who she really was inside, but she had given her what she so desperately needed at the time. She had decided to leave her fiancée, Tony, in Chicago and start a fresh life in New York. She had transferred to the New York SWAT unit from the one in Chicago and was thrown in at the deep end with the best team on the unit, Alpha team. Being on SWAT kept her busy, and up until a month ago her life revolved around her job, but then she was kidnapped and shot in her leg and so now she was taking time off to recover, and she was missing not going in and doing her job. She never thought she would feel this way about any job, but it made her feel whole and that it was worth getting out of bed each day to go and do it. Sitting around for most of the day gave her too much time to think, which was becoming an issue. She had started a relationship with her team leader, Sergeant Will Falco, and although things were OK on the surface, she had her doubts.

Now she was a sergeant too and starting her own team, their relationship had been given the green light by the captain, but it hadn't been easy. He had saved her life and caught the man that had done this to her, but he never spoke about it. He also never talked about his parents who had been shot and killed by the same man, which he himself had admitted proudly while he held her captive, though according to reports, his parents had been killed in a car accident. She had been meaning to ask him about them and which was in fact the truth, but there had never been the right time, and his reluctance to speak about it all had left her in such confusion, but Will didn't know what he had told her and so she didn't know what to say. Will worked nearly every day. He came to hers to eat and sleep and then he went back to work the next day. Before Kathy, there had been many women who were models and actresses; she had heard all the stories, and she knew they went to parties and charity dinners, but all they did was sit at her house and eat, then go to bed. She had been in a lot of pain and she wasn't walking properly yet, but they never really went anywhere or did anything together. It was sometimes like he was embarrassed by their relationship and that he didn't want the people he usually associated with to know. She had not been able to work out what had connected him to that world, mainly because his life was one big secret, and as of yet she hadn't managed to piece it all together. Maybe she should ask Will, but would he ever open up and tell her the truth if she did? All she knew was that the man who shot her was the link to so many things, but until she was back in the office, she was never going to piece it all together.

She had visitors, especially her best friend Gina who also worked in SWAT, but she worked in dispatch. She came around regularly and entertained Kathy and made her laugh so much. She was a character indeed, standing at just five feet tall; what she lacked in height she definitely made up for with her personality. Her parents were from the Caribbean, and on the occasions Kathy had met them, she knew exactly why Gina was the woman she was. They often talked about Will, but Gina never said too much which made Kathy wonder if she knew more than she was letting on. She knew that Gina and Will had dated years ago, but she also knew that Gina was exceptionally loyal and would never tell. One day last week she had mentioned that Will had changed his name when he joined the force. She hadn't noticed it came out in the conversation, but as of yet Kathy couldn't find what made that significant, though she knew it was.

The others in the team had been to visit too. Will had even organised a barbeque at the weekend so she could see everyone and socialise a little. It had made her feel a lot better as the only people she seemed to see were the physio and doctor on a regular basis except for Gina and Will.

There hadn't been much physical contact between her and Will, though she presumed it was because of her leg and nothing more but she wasn't sure. Maybe he was waiting for her in some way but the problem was there were so many doubts in her mind about where their relationship was going, and when all she had time to do was think, it was constantly playing on her mind. She had made the mistake, one day when Will was at work; she had looked on social media and, in the newspapers, and she had seen pictures of Will with so many glamorous women, and she had started to wonder about why Will wanted to be with her. Did he feel guilty about what had happened and felt he should stick with her for a while? She wondered if he would get bored and then move on with another of these women, with whom, if the pictures were anything to go by, he was having fun with, a thing that had seemed to be missing from this relationship.

She was wanting to get back to work and start getting her new team together but she knew it wouldn't be just yet: the doctors had estimated around twelve weeks before she could be back in the office and a further four weeks at least till she could be back on active duty. She was struggling to sleep though, but hadn't wanted to tell Will. Every time she closed her eyes, she saw his face, the man who shot her, pointing a gun at her. She wasn't sure how she was going to face him when it went to trial and she was hoping he would change his plea to guilty so they could all avoid going over it yet again, like the numerous times they had already gone over the facts. She was tired of reliving those days sitting in the aircraft hangar, so cold and scared; she never wanted to feel that way again.

Chapter 1

It had been twelve weeks since Kathy had been kidnapped and shot, twelve weeks that Sergeant Will Falco had been a team member down on Alpha team in NYPD's SWAT unit. Twelve weeks that he and Kathy had been together, and today Will was sitting in his office contemplating how he was going to tell her everything. He had been staying at her house to avoid the truth about who he was and now he wasn't really quite sure how to tell her. Had he left it too long? But he needed to know that it was going somewhere and would work out before he told her everything. He wasn't sleeping properly and the stress at work was worse than ever. It was normal for him to be in before his team but recently he had found himself in the office earlier than normal, trying to avoid difficult conversation with Kathy about the kidnapping and shooting.

From his office he could see the main door to the unit office and his team's desks. The SWAT offices were in the centre of Manhattan, at one of the precincts. Although it was separate, there was a dispatch office, a training room, an indoor range, a gym, the vehicle garage and gun cage. Then there was the main office. There were eight groups of five desks for the teams and then offices round the outside for the team leaders, the three lieutenants and Captain Bridge. Will's team's desks were by the door as they were called out more than all the others, but Will's office was right next to the captain's, and people said it was the only way the captain could keep an eye on him. He seemed to spend a lot of time in there especially after a call, usually because of a complaint another department had made, but the captain always had his back because he got the job done and was by far the best officer on the department but also because he knew most complaints were made out of jealousy and anger; Will was so confident in the field, it got a lot of people's backs up.

'Sergeant Falco.' The captain appeared at his door. 'You have a new team member starting today. She will be here any minute.'

'Do we have her file, so I know what I'm working with?'

'Yes, we do, she transferred from Denver, but she's quite new to SWAT.' Captain Bridge put her file on Will's desk.

'Seriously, a rookie on Alpha,' Will responded, picking it up.

'Yes, and don't be too hard, I don't have the list I used to of people wanting to work with you after the bank, so be nice.'

'I will be my usual charming self, Captain,' he replied grinning.

'That's what worries me.'

The captain walked back to his office. Just then, Will saw Tom Hargreaves walk in the office. Tom was his number two and had been his best friend since school. Will stood up and went to his door.

'Tom,' he called over to his friend.

Tom walked over; he was nearly as tall as Will who stood at six foot four, but Will had short, black hair and had a Latin appearance, taking after his Brazilian mother. Tom had brown hair but was much fairer. Both were lean and muscular. Will insisted that all the team stayed fit and in shape and he spent many hours in the gym and expected his team to do the same. They trained as a team at work, and alone in their own time just to keep up with Will.

'Morning, Will, what's up?'

'We have a new team member. When she arrives get her kitted out; she can have call sign orange, then we will see how good she is on the range, but she's a rookie so will probably need a lot of training.'

Tom turned around, and he saw a woman he didn't recognise walk in the office.

'I'm guessing that's her.'

'Yeah, I would think so,' Will replied as he glanced over. 'Let me know when you are done with the tour.'

'What's her name?'

'No clue.' Will walked behind his desk and sat down.

'OK, I will find out,' Tom said and headed over to her.

She was around five foot eleven. She had long, dark hair that had some colourful streaks in it. She was broad and quite heavy.

'Hi, I'm Officer Sara Richards, I was told to ask for Sergeant Falco.'

'I'm Officer Hargreaves, his number two. He told me to get you kitted out and give you the tour.'

'Well, I'm supposed to see the sergeant, so if you can just show me where he is then I can sort things out from there,' she replied with attitude.

'He is busy, so he has asked me to get you set up.'

'I can wait, it's fine.'

Will could hear what was going on. He stood up and came out of his office and walked over to them. He wasn't impressed.

'Is there a problem?'

'Sergeant Falco, I'm Sara Richards, your new team member.' She smiled.

Will looked her up and down.

'So why are you standing here when I told Hargreaves to get you set up and show you around?'

'I was told to report to you, Sergeant, not your number two.'

Will looked at Tom, with a look they had exchanged regularly over the years. Many recruits had come in with a similar attitude, and Will had never cared for it. On Alpha you had to prove your place, not presume you were good enough. He turned back to her.

'And now you have reported, go with him and get set up, because quite frankly I have more important things to do, and that's why it's part of my number two's job.' He started to head back towards his office, but paused and turned to look at her. 'And, by the way, I don't ever expect to have to come out here again to sort shit like this out, Richards. I suggest you get on the same page as my team and fast,' he said before going in his office and closing the door.

Richards stood and looked at his closed door for a moment and then turned to Tom who was trying his best not to laugh. It was a scenario he had seen a few times in the last eight years that Will had been in charge of Alpha, but Will seemed a little more off than usual; maybe it was because she was replacing Kathy.

'Does he talk to everyone like that?'

'Yeah, pretty much. Welcome to Alpha team.'

***

After they got back to the office, Tom introduced Sara to the rest of Alpha team: Harvey, Bennett and Palmer. Harvey was tall, African American, married to Selena and had three children. He was the one who had been with Will since he took over Alpha team. Bennett was shorter and quite stocky. Palmer was tall and thin. They were the younger ones and hadn't been on the team as long, only two years. Tom left Richards with the others and went in to see Will, closing the door behind him.

'Hey.'

'Hey, you sort everything out with our new recruit?' Will asked, briefly looking up.

'Yeah, are you OK?'

'Yeah, of course, why do you ask?'

'Because you were a little more hostile than normal before, and she didn't seem impressed either.'

Will sat back in his chair.

'I don't really care if she was impressed or not, Tom. There's something about her I don't trust.'

'You only just met her; I know it's not the same without Kathy on the team but…'

'This has nothing to do with Kathy. I have been looking at her file while you were showing her round and something doesn't add up; to get sent to us so fast after passing her entry to SWAT, and to join an Alpha team, it's not right.'

'Maybe she's that good, you were.'

'You really think she is?' Will stood up and walked round his desk. 'Does she look like she is that capable? I doubt she could run up a flight of stairs for a start. Who makes an Alpha team within two months especially in a high-profile city like this?'

'Fair point, but she could have had shooting experience before she joined, or maybe she wanted to move and ours was the only space going, and anyway, it's not our call, is it?'

'No, it's not this time, because according to the captain, no one wants to work with us after the bank incident and all that, except her. However, we can keep an eye on her till we find out more about her history and what brings her to us.'

Just then their beepers went off.

Chapter 2

The call was at a shopping mall on the edge of the city. They stopped within the police cordon and got out. Will headed over to the officer in charge. Sara went to follow him but Tom stopped her.

'The sergeant doesn't need any help getting the information, Richards. You need to get ready for when he gets back or it will be a big problem for you,' he said to her.

She got ready, all the time watching Will, and not taking her eyes off him, which Tom found a little strange. Will had a conversation with the sergeant. He got the information he needed as well as a map of the mall and headed back to the team to brief them.

'OK, we have three armed suspects in the food court with numerous hostages. The rest of the mall has been evacuated and as of yet no one has been killed though we have several with gunshot wounds. They are reported to be teenagers so let's try and get everyone out alive on this one.' Will laid out the map and showed the team the area as he spoke. 'We will be positioned on the balcony overlooking the area. When we get up there stay low or they will see us above the handrail.'

'How many hostages?' Bennett asked.

'Don't know, they are trying to talk them down. Charlie team will be on the ground floor to move in when they are clear to do so.'

They grabbed their weapons and headed towards the main doors. He put his hand on the door handle and stopped. He turned around to his team.

'Red, Green and White to fire on this and only if required to do so, and you,' he said pointing to Richards, 'you watch and learn.'

'I have done this before, Sergeant.'

'Not on my team you haven't, and from here on in that's all that matters.'

They all followed him into the mall; it wasn't too big. Charlie team went straight ahead slowly towards the food court. Sara headed for the elevators that were just to the left of the doors.

'What the hell are you doing?' Will said sternly. 'We always use the stairs no matter how many floors we are going up,' he gestured at her, 'so you may want to spend some more time in the gym.'

They all headed up the stairs; Sara followed last. She was glad there was only one flight to go up. When she planned her move to New York, she was intending to be the star of her new team, but it seemed all she had managed to do was annoy Sergeant Falco and that was really going to go against the plan. She had to make up for her bad start and show him how amazing she could be.

They came to the top of the stairs and started moving towards the food court area. When they got to the balcony area, Will signalled for the team to get down low so they wouldn't be seen from below. They positioned themselves in twos around the balcony as Will signalled to them. Richards was teamed up with Tom, and Will made sure he was at the other end. He focussed on the situation playing out before him. They were laid down on the floor, their rifles just at the edge between the barrier and the floor. They were lucky as some malls had clear barriers but this one didn't which made it easier for the team.

'Control, Alpha team in position, Red, Green and White to fire on my command. I repeat Red, Green and White to fire on my command only,' Will whispered into his radio.

'We read you Alpha team, await instruction,' came the reply.

Will watched as one of the suspects spoke on the phone to the negotiator. He was agitated and seemed angry about something though Will couldn't quite hear what he was saying. The three of them were just kids; they can't have been much more than eighteen. Will wondered what had happened in their lives to make them do something like this. A thought that often went through his mind whenever he came to a school shooting or anything that involved young people. When he was that age he only fired a gun on the range. It had been the hardest thing to do to shoot at a suspect for the first time when he joined the police department and now it happened all too often. He knew though that he had a great responsibility to save the lives of the innocent people that were always caught up in the middle of these situations, and no matter the age of the suspect, he had that to do.

One of the hostages stood and asked to allow their child to use the rest room. The suspect shouted no and pointed a gun at her and told her to sit back down. Just then a shot was fired from one of his team; it hit the counter behind the suspects. They looked up and started firing at where Will and his team were positioned; the glass above them shattered and covered the team. They were heavily armed and just kept firing. The team stayed low and the bullets went well above their heads. It wouldn't be impossible for one of them to be hit though if they lifted their head too high.

'We are under heavy fire, permission to return fire.'

'You have a green light, Alpha team, return fire!'

'Red, Green and White we have a green light, return fire.'

Three shots rang out and then everything fell silent.

'The three suspects are down; we are all clear,' Will radioed through.

'Received, Alpha team, Charlie team, you are clear to move in.'

Will got up, shook off the glass, grabbed his rifle and walked off. The team slowly followed. As they were walking out, Sara was behind the others.

'I have a feeling that we will be needing a new team member real soon,' Bennett said as he walked besides Tom.

Tom looked over his shoulder and looked at Sara; she was walking so confidently. Will was right about her, and he was worried that all this wouldn't end well.

***

The office was empty when they got back, though Will could see that Captain Bridge was in his office. Will went into his office and got his coffee cup. He came back out. The team were all sitting at their desks. He poured his coffee and then turned around to face his team. He took a drink and stood for a moment in silence looking at his team one by one. Most avoided eye contact but Richards was almost smiling. He took a deep breath before he spoke.

'So, who can tell me what went wrong on that call out?' Will asked.

He waited for a few moments to see if anyone answered.

'OK, an easier question then, hands up the three call signs that were instructed to fire on that call.'

Tom, Bennett and himself raised their hands. Will looked right at Sara.

'Did anyone hear me say ORANGE?' Will shouted.

The team shook their heads and looked at Sara.

'He pointed his gun at a hostage, and I reacted,' she replied, folding her arms defiantly.

Will put his cup down and walked right up to her.

'I'm sorry, did I miss your promotion to sergeant and the appointment of you into my job as Alpha team leader?' he asked.

'No,' she said with the same defiant attitude.

'I didn't think so, until you decided to ignore my orders. Everyone was alive, now we have three dead teenagers and several wounded hostages, all because you fired your weapon without permission, and, worst of all, you bloody missed.'

She sat in silence, not even looking up at him.

'Now, my team are the best in this state, if not the whole damn country because we work hard and train hard to be that good, and you just don't measure up to that. I don't know how you got transferred onto this team and I don't care, but I can assure you the only place you are going to fire a weapon is on the range until I say otherwise,' he crouched down to her level, 'and if you ever disobey another one of my orders you will never wear that uniform again.' He stood. 'Now get out of this office and go to the range because you have a serious amount of work to do.' He walked back over to where he had left his coffee and picked it up.

Sara stood and looked at the team, who all looked away. She walked out of the office and took out her phone and sent a text.

'We have a serious problem.'

27

Will started walking to his office, when he heard the captain shout, 'Falco, get in here.'

Will paused then headed over. As he got to the door, he shouted to Tom, 'Go and keep an eye on her, would you, Tom?'

'Sure, Sergeant, I will head down there now.'

'The rest of you get your reports written.'

Will walked into the captain's office, shut the door and sat down, taking a sip of his coffee.

'You don't like your new recruit much, do you Sergeant? I thought I had told you to be nice.'

'You did, but if I can't trust her, it's no good, Captain.'

'I told you, Falco, we are very short on options; you will have to make the best of it, till I can find someone else.'

'Unless she kills someone before then.'

'She's that bad?'

'Not only did she disobey an order, she completely missed.'

The captain sat back in his chair in complete, stunned silence, and thought for a moment. Will was drinking his coffee as they sat for several minutes.

'OK,' the captain said finally, 'give me a few weeks or so. If she still isn't up to scratch by then you can get rid of her but I need a bit of time.'

'OK, but she doesn't get a live weapon on any call at all, till I say she is up to my standard.'

'That's fair if she is partnered up or left with the vehicle at all times.'

'Deal.'

'OK, I will start looking for a new recruit.'

'A rookie? Really, Captain?'

'I am thinking they could train with Sergeant Hill and her new team then move to you after that.'

'Yeah, OK, I can work with that, as long as I have a say.'

'Well, I will have to see who will work with you but OK.'

Will got up and left and as he did, he saw Kathy crossing the office in her uniform. He met her halfway, resisting the urge to kiss her, because that's all he wanted to do but his team were sitting there. He stood right in front of her and smiled.

'So, the doctor passed you to come back?'

'To do office work and train my new team, yeah, but no calls yet. By the time they have passed though I should be fit enough,' he said.

'That's great. Listen, I have to pop down to the range to check on my new recruit, but I will be back really soon and we can have a coffee in your new office.'

'I have to see the captain anyway, so you go and do what you need to do.'

He smiled as he exited the office. Kathy turned to see the rest of Alpha team looking at her.

'Welcome back, Sergeant Hill,' Bennett said, smiling at her.

'Thanks, it's good to be back,' she said, smiling back before heading to the captain's office.

***

Down on the range Sara was at one of the firing points, and Tom was standing a few steps behind her, watching what she was doing. The range wasn't too big with only eight firing points and it was only really used for handguns. They had another training facility on the edge of the city with all other weapon ranges and assault courses, but they didn't get out there as often as Will would like and the facilities here were all they had room for. Will came in, stood next to Tom and leaned against the wall.

'So, how's it going?'

'She is all over the place, three complete misses, the rest are all in the outer rings. She's not even close.'

'Seriously, how did she even get on SWAT?'

'I don't know, because with these scores she shouldn't have.'

'Did you check her aim and position?'

'Not yet, just seeing what she got first, going to try that next.'

'Well, good news, we only have to put up with her till Kathy has trained the new recruits up and then she is gone.'

'That is good news.'

'Yeah, it is, so check her aim and stance and see if that improves it.' He moved towards the door. 'Kathy's here so I'm going back up.'

'Yeah, no worries, I'm good here.'

Will walked out, and Tom went over to Sara who was struggling to even aim at the target.

'OK, let's check your position and how you are aiming because you don't have long to get up to scratch.'

'What?'

'You can't be surprised after today, Richards, and these targets are nowhere near what we are looking for. Sergeant Falco demands the best on alpha, and if he doesn't get it then you will be leaving the team and possibly the unit, but if you work hard then you may just make it, but it's going to be a tough road.'

'I didn't have a problem in Denver. They wanted me on SWAT.'

'I don't know why with these scores, but if you listen and work hard you may just make it and stay around a bit longer. Now, show me how you aim.'

Chapter 3

Kathy was in her new office when Will got back upstairs. He got some coffee and went in. It was twice the size of Will's office with large windows making it much lighter. She had a better desk and chair and there were even a couple of large plants, which Will didn't even have space for.

'Well this is nicer than mine,' he said, putting down the cups and sitting on the edge of the desk. 'How the hell did you get this one and I'm stuck with the tiny one next to the captain?'

'Yes, it is, and I guess I'm just lucky or they don't expect me to be as much trouble as you,' she laughed.

'So how did it go with the captain?'

'Good, I have to go through these three piles of files and then choose ten officers for interview, which I have to do the day after tomorrow, and then choose my team from there. I am on a pretty short deadline to get all this done to be honest.' She put one of the files on the floor and picked up another. 'So, how did it go downstairs?'

'Well, she's as bad as I thought she was,' he stood up and walked round behind her, 'so make sure you choose me a good one,' he said, leaning over and kissing the back of her neck.

'Not here,' she said quickly. 'There will be plenty of time for that at home, and I'm not in charge of picking yours, the captain has that honour.'

'Oh yeah, he did say that it was his choice.'

'Yeah, he did.' She looked up at Will and smiled. 'Are you worried about that?'

'No, of course not, but I just think you would choose better, that's all.'

'Why, thank you.'

Just then Will's beeper went off.

'See you in a bit,' he said as he headed out.

Kathy sighed as she looked at the stack of files in front of her. She was quite nervous about starting her own team and sometimes wished things were back as they were. She sat back in her chair, holding her coffee, sipping it while contemplating. Things with Will were great, well, as good as they could be at present, but she knew he was holding back and she knew he was hiding something. She had still never been to his place, and he had still not spoken about what happened. She got up and stood at her office door for a moment, looking at the Alpha team desks, thinking about everything.

***

Will's team arrived at a block of flats in Queens. The building was quite run down and it was obvious by the people looking on that the police presence wasn't welcome. There were people round the whole of the police cordon, many with their phones out, waiting for the police to do anything they disliked so they could record it and put it on social media. The modern society and its obsession with social media had made the police look very bad so many times, and it wasn't unusual for Alpha team to be in the spotlight, but Will was trying to create a better image for the unit and he was starting with how he himself behaved in public. After the whole kidnapping and his mistake of threatening a reporter on camera, he was more aware of the whole thing and was looking to change the public perspective of the police. It was going to be a long road, that was for sure; he always had struggled with that part.

They were met by a sergeant from the local precinct, one that Will had worked with many times.

'Sergeant Falco, good to see you.'

'Sergeant Barnes, what have you got for us?'

'We have a guy in a first -floor flat, we followed him here after he fled from an armed robbery at a local pawn shop.'

'OK, so what's the play?'

'We need you to be ready if we need you to go in, but we are trying to talk him out.'

'OK, we will suit up and be ready.'

***

After an hour of waiting, Tom walked over to Will.

'So, Kathy is back, you must be happy about that.'

'Yeah, of course.'

'Is she OK now then, all healed?'

'The doctor said she can work from the office and train for now so it means she can get started on her team.'

'That's great, so have you had the conversation yet?'

'What conversation?' Will looked at him, puzzled.

'About you, you know.'

'That conversation. No, not yet, I want to but there just never seems to be the right time. I was actually planning on speaking to her tonight.'

At that moment Sara walked over to them, smiling.

'Are we just standing here all afternoon, Sergeant?'

'Why? Are you keen to get back on the range, Richards? We wait here until we are needed, or the situation is resolved and we won't be needed at all. Now go and stand with Palmer, he is your partner on this one.'

She walked off and went and stood with Palmer.

'You don't like her, do you?'

'I don't know her well enough not to like her but I don't trust her.'

'Well, with a bit of luck the captain will find us a decent new recruit.'

'I am sure he will.'

***

It was three hours later when they finally got back to the office. They had been standing there all that time and, in the end, he had given himself up, so as far as Will was concerned, it was a good afternoon. It was unusual for them to wait so long and not be sent in; most precincts would have sent them in after thirty minutes and forced the suspect out. Will was glad they didn't as it always seemed to make SWAT look trigger-happy when they did. Kathy was on the phone, and so Will grabbed a coffee and headed towards his own office. He was ready to finish up and go home, but had some paperwork to sign off. Just then Sara appeared at his door.

'Sergeant, we are all heading over the road for a drink. Do you want to come?'

'Another night, Richards.'

'Come on, Sergeant, it is the end of my first shift. I know I really messed up but I really want to learn and work hard to be just as good as you and the others here.'

Will sat back in his chair and looked at her. He was really struggling to weigh her up and figure out what she was doing here.

'OK, but let me tell Sergeant Hill.'

'She can come to if she wants to. It will be nice to get to know everyone in a more relaxed place.' She smiled.

'OK, we will be over soon.'

Sara walked out of the office with a big smile on her face.

***

'I thought you didn't like her and now we are going for a drink with her,' Kathy said as they crossed the road to the Charlie's bar.

'I know, but I want to try and get a read on her and after a beer or two she maybe open enough for me to do that.'

'OK, but I wanted a quiet night in to be honest. I have a lot of work to do for these interviews.'

'I know, we can just have one maybe two and go early. I wanted to talk to you about something anyway.'

'Sounds good to me, let's get this over with,' Kathy said as she opened the door.

Charlie's bar was a popular spot for officers as it was just over the road from the precinct. It was a long room with a bar that stretched virtually the whole way down. There were plenty of tables and chairs and bar stools in the window and by the bar. Charlie was usually behind the bar in the evening, especially on the busier nights. The team was sitting at the far end of the bar near the pool table. Will went to the bar, and Kathy went and sat down next to Tom.

'Hey, Kathy, how's it going?'

'Good, thanks, Tom, better now I'm back at the office even if I'm stuck behind a desk.'

'Wasn't sure we would see you two in here tonight, to be fair, thought you would head straight home.'

'Yeah, me too but Will said he should come by so here we are, and we haven't been out since the shooting so it's OK.'

Will came and sat down next to Kathy with two drinks. Just then Sara came and sat on the other side of Will; she was followed by Bennett and Palmer. Harvey had gone straight home as Selena had called and said one of the kids was ill.

'So, do we still have to call you Sergeant out of work?' Sara asked flirtatiously.

Will looked at her suspiciously. He wasn't sure why she was being so friendly, and she was completely different to how she had been earlier.

'No, you can call me Falco.'

Tom and Kathy tried their best not to laugh.

'No first names? Not even outside work?' she asked, almost confused.

'The only people who call me by my first name are Tom because we have known each other since school and my beautiful Sergeant Hill here,' he replied quite sternly.

'Yeah, Falco here never calls us by our first names and vice versa,' Bennett chipped in.

'But that's so impersonal,' Richards said, disappointed.

'That's OK because I don't ever want to be that personal with you, Richards.'

Sara sat back in her chair for a moment. This wasn't exactly having the effect that she had wanted. She needed to get close to him and he just wasn't open to that. She looked at Kathy. Maybe if she could separate them, she could get closer.

'So, Falco, is it true you used to date models and actresses?'

'What does that matter?'

'Just what I heard so I was curious, that's all.'

Kathy and Tom looked at each other, trying to work out where she was going with this and how it was a relevant or appropriate conversation to be having.

'Yeah, he did.' Bennett interrupted the moment of silence. 'Our sergeant is a serious stud in those circles, always going to functions with a beautiful lady on his arm, and rarely the same one for more than a month.'

'Really?' Sara smiled. 'Well, you know there are only two reasons a man has women like that queueing up.' She looked at Will and smiled. 'Money or amazing sex.'

Palmer nearly choked on his drink, Kathy sat back in shock and Will exchanged a look with Tom. Kathy saw it and wondered how many of these looks she had missed before.

'Well, it can't be money because sergeants don't get paid that much, do they?' Bennett said.

'No, sergeants don't get paid that much,' Sara replied, smiling at Will.

'I think this conversation has gone far enough,' Will said. 'My past relationships are quite frankly none of your business, Richards, and they are exactly that, in the past.'

Sara knew she had hit a nerve so she decided to change the subject quickly and try something else, though looking at Kathy's face, it may still have done enough damage.

'OK, my apologies, anyone fancy a game of pool?'

Bennett and Palmer both stood up. Tom shook his head as did Kathy.

'Come on, Sergeant, just one game?' Bennett asked

Will looked at Kathy and she nodded.

'OK, just one game.' He stood and took his jacket off; his T-shirt was tight and Kathy saw Richards look him up and down as they headed towards the table. Kathy took a drink and turned to Tom.

'So, will you tell me because I know Will won't.'

'Tell you what?'

'What that look was about before between you two, what he's hiding, why he never talks about his family and his past.'

Tom looked at her and sighed.

'Kathy, as much as I love you it's just not my place.'

'But you know.'

'We were at school together, I know everything.'

'So why won't he tell me?'

'He said he was going to tell you tonight, but then you showed up here.'

'Richards,' she said, looking over at them.

Richards was obviously flirting with him, though he wasn't showing any interest except in the game. She wasn't a match for him, but Kathy wasn't sure she was either.

'He's not interested in her.'

'I know, but I don't exactly match up to his past girlfriends, do I?'

'You beat them all.'

'I doubt that.' She sighed. 'Truth is I'm not sure how I feel about it all.'

'Kathy, he adores you, it's just he has been hurt so much before.'

'Haven't we all.'

'Look, let him explain it all and I know you will see it all different.'

Kathy looked at Will and had a big drink. She stood up.

'I'm going home. This was a mistake. Tell Will I will see him tomorrow. I need to clear my head.'

She walked out before Tom could respond. About five minutes later Will looked over, saw she wasn't there and walked over to Tom.

'Where's Kathy?'

'She's gone home.'

'What!' He put his jacket on. 'What did she say?'

'That this was a mistake, that she would see you tomorrow, and she needed to clear her head.'

Will grabbed his helmet and started to head for the door.

'Will, maybe you should leave it tonight.'

Will looked at Tom for a moment then walked out.

'Where's the sergeant going?' Sara asked as she walked over. 'We are in the middle of a game.'

'He's gone home,' Tom replied.

Chapter 4

Will was sitting on his motorcycle with his helmet off when Kathy arrived in a taxi. She looked over at him and then walked up her steps towards her front door.

'Kathy,' he called, getting off his motorcycle.

Kathy continued to the top without even looking round at him, and unlocked the door.

'Kathy!' he shouted as he followed her up the steps.

She turned around and slowly walked down three steps, and stopped.

'What was that about?'

'What?'

'Leaving the bar without a word.'

'You were having fun, and I wanted to come home.'

'I would have brought you if you had said something.'

'I needed some space. I told Tom I would see you tomorrow.'

'Yeah, he said, space from me? And what was the mistake?'

'Space from you, from everything.'

'I don't understand.'

Kathy sat on the steps. Will walked up a few more so he could look into her eyes.

'I don't think I'm ready.'

'Ready for what?' he asked cautiously.

'For us,' she replied sadly.

They both looked at each other for a moment before she continued.

'Tonight, I realised that all those women are so beautiful and you chose me when I don't even match up.'

'You don't have to.'

'And people will always look at me and wonder why you settled for less, like they did tonight.'

'Are you seriously saying this? It doesn't matter what the likes of Richards thinks, she is not important and why are you so fixated on the past? It doesn't matter.'

'It matters to me.'

'Why?'

'You don't let me in. You never talk to me about your parents, growing up and what happened to them. You don't talk about me getting taken and being shot. You just shut me out. Like you don't trust me enough to let me in.'

'I don't talk about it with anyone. I don't see the point, if something is in the past then why keep bringing it up?'

'You always talk to Tom and even Gina knows more about your past than me.'

'Tom is literally my oldest friend. He was with me through it all, he actually lived it with me, and Gina, we dated years ago, but she doesn't know everything,' he replied defensively.

'And no one else knows?'

'I don't understand what that has to do with anything.'

'Because we have been together for three months. I have never been to your place; I don't even know where it is. You don't talk to me. How can I be with you as your partner and girlfriend if you don't trust me.'

'I do trust you.'

'But you would rather go and have drinks in a bar with Richards, who you claim you don't even like or trust, than come home and talk to me about you.'

Will looked at her questioningly.

'Tom told me.'

'Yeah and I was going to tell you everything, but this right here is why I didn't. You judge me for not opening up and telling you but when have you ever spoken about your parents and what happened with your ex to bring you here. They don't like your job but there has to be more than that.' He was getting angry.

'This is not about me, Will.'

'No, of course not because God forbid you should be in the wrong about anything.'

'That's not fair, Will.' She was obviously upset.

Will turned and started walking back down the steps, he turned around at the bottom and looked at her.

'So that's it, we're done.'

Kathy nodded. Will turned, got on his motorcycle and rode off. Kathy sat with tears rolling down her cheeks; she hadn't wanted to do that.

***

When Will got around the corner, he pulled up, took off his helmet and got his cell phone out. He made a call.

'Hi are you free?'

'Yeah, sure, where do you want to meet?' replied a woman's voice.

'Our usual place.'

'OK, I can be there in fifteen.'

Will rode to a quiet spot by the river. He got off his motorcycle and walked over to a bench, taking his helmet off and then he sat and waited, looking at the water. He loved the quietness of this spot. He wasn't sure what he had done or why Kathy had ended it but his head was a mess and he had to call the one woman he could always rely on to be there, like she had been for virtually his whole life, just like Tom. A taxi pulled up behind him.

'Hi, stranger,' she said as she got out.

'Hey, Ash, how are you?' he said, walking over and kissing her on the cheek.

'Better than you it looks,' Ashleigh answered.

She was nearly as tall as Will. She was slim with long, flowing chestnut hair and big blue eyes. She was a very successful actress and model, and she was stunning.

They walked over to the bench and sat down.

'So, what's up? Not like you to call so late on a work night.'

He leaned forward and took a deep breath; he turned his head to look at her.

'Kathy finished it and I haven't got a clue why. Then I got mad and made it worse.'

'What, I thought it was going well, from what you said the other day, anyway.'

'So did I, in fact, I was planning on telling her everything, but tonight we went for a drink after shift and something changed.'

Ashleigh moved so she was turned towards him and put her hand on his shoulder.

'OK, talk me through it.'

'Well, I got a new team member and she asked everyone to go for a drink. Her and Bennett were asking me about past relationships, then I played some pool. Kathy left, I followed and then she said she wasn't ready and ended it.'

'Your past relationships?'

'Richards, the new one, asked if I really had dated models and actresses, though I'm not sure where she heard it from. Bennett said I had and so they started to speculate as to why they had gone out with me.'

'Well, I have to say it sounds to me like she wants a bit of her sergeant.'

'What! No way.'

'Will, honey, I'm afraid it's true.'

'That explains the interest, I guess.'

He sat back on the bench and sighed, looking out at the water.

'Then you spoke to Kathy later.'

'Yeah, outside hers. She said she couldn't compare to who I had been out with before. I said she didn't have to and…'

'You said what?' she interrupted.

'That she didn't have to.' Will looked confused. 'What's wrong with that?' he asked, looking at her a little confused.

'Really? You don't know?' She paused. 'To say you have been out with so many, you are not very good with women, are you?'

'Obviously not, guess I never needed to know about these inner feelings before.'

'Yeah, that's true, since the gold digger you have been a bit of a bed hopper.'

'Wow, thanks for that, love you too, Ash.'

'Well it's true, but anyway you basically told Kathy she doesn't need to be as good as your exes.'

'What? I meant she is better than them all.'

'But that's not what you said.'

'Great, no wonder she was so mad.'

'And then you got mad?'

'Yeah, she pushes me about my past then shuts off when I ask about hers. I lost my cool and called her on it.'

'Not the best idea but I know a few ways you can work it out if you want to. So, you going to give me a lift, can go back to yours and have a drink and a chat.'

'OK, but not too late. I have work in the morning and some damage control to do, it would seem.'

They walked over to his motorcycle. Will got out his spare helmet, but she refused to put it on, so he put it away and they got on.

'I will pay the fine if we get stopped.'

'You know I'm a cop and will get in deep shit if we get pulled over.'

'Yeah, so don't go slow enough to get pulled over.'

They set off. As they did so they were followed by a car, but neither of them noticed at first. The driver took a picture of Ashleigh as she held onto Will tightly at a set of lights. The car pulled in and took a picture as they entered the garage and then as they walked into the building. When they got up to Will's apartment Ashleigh headed straight for the sofa and put her feet up, and Will went and poured them both a drink. As he sat, he handed her one.

'I swear someone took a picture of me at those last set of lights, from that car next to us.'

'Another reason to wear a helmet.'

'Normally though it would be on social media by now but there's nothing.'

'Maybe they didn't take one then.'

'Maybe, we will see in the morning no doubt.'

They sat chatting for a couple of hours before going to bed. Ashleigh had stayed over so often she had a room she considered hers.

The man taking pictures was waiting for them to reappear the next morning to take some more as they headed off to work.

Chapter 5

Will walked into the office and poured himself a coffee. He saw Kathy sitting in her office. She had started early to get stuff organised because she needed to arrange all the interviews of the officers for her new team, and be ready for the next day. She had chosen twelve which was more than she was told but she was struggling to narrow it down without meeting them. Will knocked and opened the door. She didn't look up, but knew it was him.

'I am not choosing your new team member so you will have to speak to the captain. I told you that yesterday,' she said harshly.

'I was actually wondering if we could talk about last night,' Will answered gently.

'I have nothing else to say to you, Sergeant, so if you will excuse me, I have a lot of work to do.'

'Fine.' Will walked off and into his office, slamming the door behind him. Kathy jumped. Will's team walked in the office at that moment and wondered what was going on. They started to get their coffees when their beepers went off. Will came out of his office.

'We have an armed suspect in a motel, so let's go.'

The team followed him out.

Will got out of the truck. He walked over to the waiting cars and spoke to a detective. Will had met him before and didn't like him much. He was the type of person who really didn't appreciate or respect Will and his team. He thought as a detective he was better than anyone in uniform, and he and Will had fallen out on several occasions before.

'He is in room 308, but we need this guy alive. We need him to answer some questions on a murder, so can we do that, Sergeant?'

'Well that all depends on him, but I will do my best.'

Will went over to the team and explained how they were going to go in.

'Tom, you come up with me. The rest of you can stay down here and cover the outside of the building in case he tries to escape. Richards, you can stay with the truck and observe. See if you can learn something.'

Tom followed Will up a flight of metal stairs that were at the end of the building, and they walked cautiously down to the door they wanted. They glanced through the window and they could see just one person inside. Tom kicked the door in and Will went in first.

'NYPD, put the gun down.'

There was a white male standing at the other side of the room, pointing a gun at them. He was very untidy, and looked like he may have been drinking.

'Put the gun down,' Will insisted.

He fired in Tom's direction. Will fired, hitting him in the arm. He fired again, this time towards Will. Will fired again and hit him in the head.

'Control, this is Alpha team, the suspect is down and we are all clear,' Tom radioed through.

They walked back down the stairs and started walking towards the truck.

'Hey, Sergeant!' Detective Shalt shouted after him.

Will stopped and turned around.

'I thought I said I wanted him alive. He can't answer any questions now.'

'Tried that, didn't work.'

'It wasn't for you to try, it was for you to do, Sergeant.'

'Well, he fired at me and Hargreaves, he only just missed us. I wasn't going to let him try a third time and potentially injure or kill one of us, Detective.'

'I don't care if he shot at you and every other member of your team, that's what you are paid for. Next time just do your job.'

Will passed his weapon to Tom. He pushed the detective up against a nearby car.

'Never tell me how to do my job, and next time you want cops for your suspects to use for target practice, go in your damn self and don't bother calling us.'

Will let him go and went back to the truck. The team got in without saying a word and they headed back to the PD. Will was quiet all the way back and headed upstairs when they got back. He walked straight into his office without even looking in Kathy's direction. Tom followed him.

'What was that about?'

'You heard him, Tom, expecting us to get shot at for him. What if one of them had actually hit one of us?'

'That's not what I mean, Will. You haven't reacted like that for months, and I'm guessing it has something to do with Kathy.'

Will sat on his desk and sighed loudly.

'She finished it, no explanation and now she won't even speak to me.'

'Oh, that's really rough, I'm sure when she has had some space you can sort it out.'

'Maybe, I don't know.'

'Falco, get in here!' they heard the captain shout from his doorway.

'Great that's all I need,' Will said as he left his office. He went into the captain's office closing the door behind him.

'Falco, I thought you had started playing nice with others.'

Will stood by the door and folded his arms. He wasn't in the mood for this though he knew he was pushing his luck when he reacted the way he did.

'I was till that poor excuse for a detective decided it's OK for a suspect to shoot at us and expect us to do nothing.'

'I get that, but did you really need to pin him up against a car?'

'Yeah, I know, it was a step too far, Captain, but he pissed me off with his attitude.'

'Well I really enjoyed the break, Falco, and now I am back to having other departments on my case about you. So, do you want to tell me what happened with you and Sergeant Hill that has suddenly upset the harmony in my unit.'

'We split up last night.'

'So, should I expect more of this, my phone ringing off the hook again like before?'

'No, I will resist the urge to hit or shoot someone, I'm good.'

'You sure? I can't have these problems again, Falco. You have pushed this PD to the limit, and I have always kept your past and things quiet and have protected your ass but I can't keep doing it. I have had IAB on my back and other departments asking questions about you on the back of the bank and reporter incident; it seems that people think you got off too easy. So, if you are back to your old ways, I may have to put you at your desk.'

'I get it, Captain, I'm sorry for all the problems I have caused you in the past but I will try harder and you won't regret keeping me around.'

'Good, now go and write your reports and make sure you and Hargreaves get everything straight on the shoot and what was said after. Let's see if I can't get this put to bed quickly.'

'Yes, Captain.'

Will left, went back into his office, closing the door. He sat at his desk and put his head in his hands. He needed to sort himself out: he couldn't go back to how he was. He could see, after being with Kathy and being happy, that it was no way to be. The anger over his parents had eaten away at him for far too long. He still blamed himself for their deaths. He had caught the man that shot them but it still hadn't eased the grief, and he just didn't understand why. At least with Kathy, he had been happy and been able to move forward, but now he wasn't sure what to do.

***

While Will was in with the captain, Tom decided to speak to Kathy. He knew Will would kill him if he knew what he was about to do. He knocked on her door and went in, closing it again behind him.

'I'm guessing you know, Tom, but it isn't going to make any difference, whatever you are going to say,' Kathy stated, putting her pen down and looking up at him.

'I just wanted to know why, because Will doesn't have a clue,' he said as he sat down in the chair opposite her.

'Because he is hiding things from me, because of his dating history and because he doesn't trust me enough.'

'Well, you can't use his dating history. You knew all about that from being on the team. I mean Bennett never shut up about it.'

'I only knew bits of it, not the same thing.'

'He is devastated over this, proper flipped out at a detective this morning, nearly punched him.'

'Nothing new there. How many times has that happened before, and if he was that devastated then why did he have another woman stay last night?'

'What?' Tom looked shocked.

Kathy pulled out her phone and showed Tom the pictures taken the night before and this morning of Will and Ashleigh that were now all-over social media.

'That's Ashleigh.'

'I know who she is, Tom. She is a famous actress, and, believe it or not I do have a life outside this place.'

'They have been friends since they were kids. We all hung out together when Ash was home from boarding school. She is like a little sister to Will.'

'Oh.' She put her phone away. 'I didn't know that.'

'See he only wants you.'

'Don't you see the fact I didn't know is part of the problem, because he is still keeping secrets, Tom, including the fact he lives on Park Avenue and that Ashleigh is a close friend. I mean, should his girlfriend not know things like that, and I can't be in a relationship where I don't have all the facts.'

Just then Tom's beeper went off. As he came out of Kathy's office, he walked into Will.

'Wondered where you had gone.'

They headed out. Kathy decided to investigate herself what Will was hiding, and she knew just where to start. She wasn't sure if she would like what she found but she needed to know.

Chapter 6

The call was at a warehouse. The area was really quiet but, as they arrived, they could see squad cars surrounding the building. Will got out and made his way over to the officer in charge, and as he did so shots were fired towards them from inside. Will ran back to the truck and the team got suited up very quickly. The officers were hiding behind their vehicles as bullets rained down on them. Will grabbed his rifle and looked to see if he could get a clear shot at whoever was firing at them.

'Control, we are under fire from suspects inside the warehouse. Have we a green light to proceed as necessary?'

'Alpha team, you have a green light to proceed.'

'Tom, can you see anyone, because I have got nothing, can't see anyone.'

'No, got nothing, Sergeant.'

'OK, we are going to have to get inside and find these bastards, so Harvey and Richards provide cover fire.'

'Sergeant, I only have blanks!' Richards shouted.

'They don't know that, do they? Then we will move forward and get them from the inside. We don't know how many there are so we need to clear every inch of the place before PD take it over.'

There was a pause in the gunfire so Will decided to take the chance and get inside.

'Control, this is Alpha team, we are going to enter the building. The suspects inside have paused in their fire upon us.'

'Received, Alpha team, proceed with caution.'

Will and the team broke cover and moved towards the building. They got halfway and the suspects started firing again, but stopped when Harvey and Richards returned fire. Harvey hit one of the suspects. The others got to the door. They went in together and broke off into twos; Bennett was with Will and Palmer followed Tom down the other side. They moved slowly and steadily. As they got halfway down the building, they came under fire again from three suspects. Will took one, then the others stopped and ran towards the other end of the building. The team followed in hope they would force them out into the open.

'Blue and Orange, get yourselves to the back of the building. They are heading out.'

'Received, we are on our way.'

Harvey ran down to the other end of the building. Richards was left a way behind. Harvey met the two suspects as they exited.

'NYPD, stop and put your weapons down.'

The suspects gave up as Will and the others arrived from inside the building.

'Well done, Harvey.'

Just then Richards arrived out of breath. Will walked over to her.

'You need to learn how to keep up, Richards.'

They took the two suspects to the waiting PD and went back to the truck. Richards was trailing behind, still fighting to catch her breath. Will and Tom leaned against the truck, watching her.

'She can't even run a few metres without nearly passing out. How the hell did she pass the force basic training?'

'Tom, I have no clue, but she is staying with the truck from now on because this is going to risk lives. If those guys had not given up Harvey could have had a bullet in him. Let's get back and take another look at Officer Richards.'

***

The team were exhausted when they came back in. Another three calls followed, one after another, without a break at all, and they had got back after the end of shift. Will went into his office and spotted a sheet of paper on his desk with a note on it.

'At least I know what you were hiding now,' he read aloud.

He looked at the sheet of paper. It was a picture of him at his parents' funeral. It was the article published saying they had died tragically but it didn't mention the robbery, and it didn't say in the article what his name was, just that he was their son. Kathy had found this.

'Shit,' he muttered, then punched the filing cabinet.

Tom came in. Will handed him the paper. Tom read it and closed the door.

'Kathy left that on my desk.'

'How did she find it?'

'I don't know, only three people in this department know.'

'Me, the captain and…'

'Gina.'

'She never said anything before, why now?'

'I don't know if she did say anything or maybe she let something slip, but Kathy found this and that means others can too.'

Will walked out. He needed to speak to Kathy.

***

Kathy poured two glasses of wine and brought them over, putting them on the coffee table. She sat at the opposite end of the sofa to Gina. She had needed a friend and some wine after the day she had experienced.

'So, did you find what you were looking for earlier?'

'Yeah, I did and more besides, I'm sorry I put you on the spot by asking you about Will's past.'

'It's OK, but you understand why I couldn't say anything, right?'

'Yeah, of course, just like Tom couldn't.'

'So, you found out everything?'

'I don't know, but I found some things I didn't know.'

'Is that a good thing?'

'Well, I found out who his parents were and I guess that's why it's all such a big secret though I'm not sure why.'

'So, what now, are you going to talk to him?'

'I sort of left a note on his desk with an article about his parents' funeral.'

'You serious?'

'Yeah, why?'

'Do you know Will Falco at all? He isn't going to be thrilled that you found that info and he won't be happy you called him out on it.'

'Well, no, probably not.' She stood and went over to the window. 'But he should have told me then I wouldn't have had to find anything.'

Just then they heard a motorcycle outside; it was Will. He took his helmet off, got off his motorcycle and headed up the steps. Kathy hid behind the blinds.

'It's Will, what do I do now?'

'Well, maybe you should talk to him.'

'I was planning on waiting a while, like a week or two.'

'Well, no time like the present.' Gina stood, picked up her bag and headed to the door. Kathy followed.

'What are you doing?'

'I'm leaving and letting you talk, but let me know how it goes.'

Gina opened the door. Will was just about to knock. Gina smiled as she walked past Will, and she headed off down the steps. Kathy signalled for him to go inside; he did. She closed the door and followed him through to the living room/kitchen.

'So,' he said as he stopped just inside the door way, 'you know.'

'Yeah.'

'Did you tell anyone?'

'No, and I won't so you don't have to worry about that.' She looked at him. 'It wasn't that easy to find either, if it wasn't for knowing small details I wouldn't have.'

'So, what now?' he asked as he sat on the sofa. 'Now you know.'

'If you mean us, I don't know, because I know who your parents were but that's all I know.'

'What do you want to know?'

Kathy walked over to the chair by the window and sat on it.

'How you became a cop would be a good place to start, because I'm sure there were plenty of other options for you.'

'That's easy. I hated private school and after I got kicked out of two, I went to a local one. I met Tom and his dad was a cop. When I told my parents, they thought it was great and really encouraged me and they backed me one hundred percent. My dad took me to a gun club and got me the best instructor. He had a philosophy: whatever you do in life, be the best, so when I joined SWAT, he was really proud.'

'Well that makes sense. I mean, you are the best on the unit and you try and make the team have that same belief.'

'Yeah, my dad was the best at making you feel you can do anything.'

'So why change your name?'

'My parents insisted on it; they wanted to protect me. They felt if I had their name, I would become a target in more ways than one, so I took my mom's maiden name.'

'But what about all the women? How do they not know?'

'My lovely ex-fiancée was silenced by lawyers and the rest: some didn't know my parents so it was easy to not tell them everything.'

'Ex-fiancée?'

'Yeah, my parents wanted a pre-nup. She said if I loved her, I didn't need one. When they died, she thought I would give her what she wanted. When I didn't, she left me.'

'And the rest came after, but you live on Park Avenue, does that not give it away?'

'Some know I inherited the apartment and that they had money but never knew the extent of that, and others knew my parents, and come from wealthy families themselves, but they move in circles that don't gossip about those kinds of things outside of their circle.' He paused and looked at her. 'How do you know I live on Park Avenue?'

'I saw the pictures of you and Ashleigh on social media.' She stood and moved to the window. 'Tom said you were all friends since you were kids. That made no sense at first, but now I know how that came about. It's well publicised she comes from money and so do you, though I have never heard you mention her before, which is odd considering how close you are.'

'It would create a lot of questions if people knew we grew up together. Most people think we met at a charity event, but she lived nearby. Our parents were friends, so we grew up together. Her parents still live a few blocks from me. I have known her longer than I have known Tom, actually.'

'So, what are you worth?'

'What?' He stood up. 'What does that matter?'

'It doesn't, I guess, I'm just curious. I mean, I have never known anyone that is really wealthy before.'

'Well, my family's business was very successful. When it was taken over, I made a lot of money.'

'So, millions then?'

Will walked towards the kitchen.

'At the last report, including assets which is mainly property, it was a little over twelve billion.' He didn't look at her as he said it.

'Twelve billion, are you serious? Well, now things are starting to make sense.'

Will turned around and looked at Kathy.

'What do you mean by that?'

'Why you can do anything with no consequences: all the glamorous parties and the endless women.'

'You think I bribe the captain?'

'No, I never said that, but he knows, so he will protect you, right?'

'You actually believe that we are corrupt?' he snapped.

'Yes, no, I don't know.'

'How can you even think that? I do my job through choice to make a difference, not for money or status.'

'I know money influences a lot of things, and you can't deny that.'

'Which is why I spent most of my life away from it. I hated the life where money was everything. I work my ass off to be me, a person not controlled by money and I hate people knowing because they change. The captain knows my past and keeps it quiet as does the chief but no money is involved in that. It was agreed when I joined the force and SWAT. If you honestly think I am corrupt because I have money, then you don't know me at all.'

'Maybe I don't know you. I only know the you that you allow me to know and it's not a surprise that people change. Most people can't imagine having what you have.'

'I am not the money I have and I thought you would see that.'

'I'm sorry, it's not that simple now.'

He walked over to her. She turned to face him. He stopped so close to her.

'So, what now?'

Her heart started beating faster as she felt his breath on her cheek. She wanted him so much. He leaned down and kissed her; she sank into it savouring his touch. Then suddenly she pulled away. He looked at her, but she looked away.

'I can't, Will, the truth changes everything.'

'It doesn't change who I am or how I feel about you.'

'Of course, it changes who you are.'

'No, it only changes how you see me and I can't do anything about that.'

He walked out, slamming the front door as he left. She went and sat on the sofa, and, as she heard him ride off on his motorcycle, tears ran down her cheeks. Had she just made the biggest mistake of her life? She loved him and she was going to let this ruin that.

Chapter 7

The next morning Will was sitting on Tom's desk as the team arrived. He had got there early and already had his coffee. He was smiling, holding a pile of papers.

'Good morning, everyone, today is a new day and we start with training. Dispatch have us down for emergencies only, as Charlie team are on shift. So take a seat.'

They all sat down at their desks, looking at each other as they did so. Will handed out the papers.

'Now, you need to answer all the questions, no conferring. Tom, you will keep an eye on them. I am going down to the gym for a workout. Today we all get back to being one hundred percent except Richards, of course, because you aren't even there yet, but for the rest of us, there will be no more excuses.'

He went into his office, picked up a towel and drink bottle and headed for the door. Kathy entered as he got there.

'Good morning, Sergeant Hill,' he said as he passed her.

'He seems rather cheerful this morning,' Bennett said.

'Yeah, so let's get these done and keep him that way,' Tom said as he stood and walked over to Kathy's door. He knocked and stepped in.

'So, did you two work it out?'

'We talked but we aren't back together. Why?'

'Oh, because Will is really cheerful so I thought you must have.'

'No, so whatever or whoever made him so happy, it wasn't me.'

***

Will had been working out for about forty minutes when his beeper went off. He picked up his towel and wiped himself down, then grabbed his drink bottle and shirt and went upstairs at a quick pace.

'What we got, Tom?' he asked as he walked into the office.

'School shooting, Sergeant.'

'Great, I hate those. Let me grab a clean shirt. Grab your gear and I will meet you downstairs at the truck.'

Will went in his office, got a fresh shirt and put it on while heading towards the door.

'Officer Barnes,' Kathy said to the female officer sitting outside her door.

'What?' She looked at Kathy once Will had gone.

'Officer Barnes, do you want to come in?'

She got up and followed Kathy into her office. Kathy closed the door behind her.

'Do all SWAT officers look like that?' she asked as she sat down.

'I'm sorry, look like what?'

'Like that, all muscly and toned.'

'No, just Sergeant Falco.'

'That's Sergeant Falco, wow he is better looking than I thought he would be.' She looked at Kathy. 'You know he is a legend in the fifteenth precinct, for his shooting as well as his looks.'

'Right, so why do you want to join SWAT?'

'Will we be working closely with his team, because I would sure love that, I mean, who wouldn't?'

'Officer Barnes, the team will only work with Alpha when we are needed to, not all the time.'

'Oh, but he will be training us though, right?'

'No, I will be training you.'

'Well, I know it's your team but he's the best so thought he would be helping sometimes at least.'

'OK, well, I think that's all for now. Thanks for coming in.'

'Right, OK.' She stood up and left.

Kathy got up and went out to grab a coffee before her next recruit arrived. The captain was getting one too.

'Sergeant Hill, how are the interviews going?'

'Well the last one was more interested in Sergeant Falco walking round half naked than joining my team,' she answered while pouring her coffee.

'Well, I'm sure not all of them will be interested in that. I mean most applicants are men, right,' he joked.

70

'Probably not but who knows.' She smiled. 'Do we know how it's going at the school?'

'Not really, seems they are trying to get the suspect to talk, but struggling to get through. Falco is clearing the school and as they do so they are trying to locate him and the hostages.'

'Well, I'm sure it will work out.'

***

Will and his team were suited up and ready to go.

'OK, Sergeant Falco, we need you to go in at the entrance and work your way room by room down each corridor and clear the building. We believe he is in the sports hall with some hostages, but we need to make sure.'

'We are on it, no problem. Harvey with me, Tom you take Bennett and Palmer. Richards, you get to stay here with the truck.'

'Why?'

'You need to ask that, after the shopping mall and the warehouse? Right, guys, let's go.'

Richards watched as they walked off into the school, furious at being embarrassed in front of the other officers. She knew they were looking at her. She got back in the truck before anyone said anything to her and got out her cell phone. She needed to work a few things out.

The team went in the main doors and then worked their way down the corridor, checking each classroom as they went on either side. The sports hall was at the end. Will signalled to the team to stay back from the door while he got a visual. He saw the suspect inside, and he had two handguns pointing at a group of teenagers in sports uniforms. Will stepped back and radioed through.

'Control, we have the suspect in the sports hall. You can send Charlie team in to clear the rest of the building.'

'Received, Alpha team, can you get a clear shot?'

'Not without entering the sports hall, there are around ten hostages.'

'Received, stand by.'

Will waited for instruction and kept his team back; they couldn't risk being seen by the suspect as it could threaten the lives of those inside.

'Alpha team, you are clear to go in and use any force necessary.'

'Alpha team received.'

Will signalled to Tom.

'They want us to go in.'

'So what's the plan?'

'I think it's best if you, me and Harvey go in and Bennett and Palmer cover the door. We go in and try and talk him out but stay aimed, he has more than one weapon.'

'Sounds good to me.'

'Control, Alpha team positioned and ready; Red, Green and Blue to enter, White and Yellow to cover the door.'

'Received, Alpha team, you have a green light.'

They opened the door gently and slowly entered the hall. They moved as quietly as possible and didn't announce themselves till they were level with the suspect.

'NYPD, put your weapons down and get down on the ground,' Will said loudly.

The suspect spun round quickly and looked at them in shock. He waved his guns around as he spoke.

'Stop there or I will shoot them. You aren't supposed to be here. No one is supposed to be here except for them.'

'Well, when someone starts shooting in this city, we usually show up. That's what we do, but we want everyone to walk out of here,' Will responded.

'You don't understand. These people made my life hell; they laughed at me, pulled cruel pranks on me and bullied me every single day. They made me want to die.' He was clearly upset and emotional.

Tom moved forward and started to lower his weapon.

'Listen, my name is Tom, what's yours?'

'Ryan.'

'Ryan, I've been where you are, bullied and made to feel like an outsider, rich kids making you feel worthless. I get it, I really do but this isn't the answer.'

'I just wanted them to stop.'

'I know, I get that, but if you fire at one of them then my sergeant here will shoot you, then they win, they all win.'

Tom stepped forward, mirrored by Will on his left. Harvey stayed closer to the door.

'Give me the guns, Ryan, and let's walk out of here, go somewhere else to school. You haven't hurt anyone yet so it's not serious.'

'Really, I just wanted them to stop. I thought if I scared them, they would leave me alone.'

Tom moved forward. He put out his hand to take one of the guns. He could see tears in the boy's eyes. He took one gun and put it in his belt. He was about to take the other when one of the hostages jumped up and grabbed it, pointing it at Ryan and Tom.

'Ryan, move behind me quickly.'

Ryan did what Tom asked and they started to move backwards towards the door. Will didn't move.

'No, he needs to stay where he is. He doesn't get to come in here, point a gun at us and walk out.'

'Sergeant, have you got him?' Tom asked.

'Yes, I do.'

He spun round to face Will.

'You need to put your gun down, Officer, because unlike him I'm not scared of you, because I know you can't shoot me.'

'Yeah, that's not going to happen because in fact I am permitted to fire, and it's Sergeant not Officer.'

'Harvey, get Ryan out of here!' Tom shouted.

Harvey moved forward, gun on the new suspect, took Ryan to the door and out, shielding him the whole way.

'No, bring him back here,' the new suspect shouted.

'No, he is gone, so you can put that down,' Tom said to him.

The suspect moved towards Tom, then he pulled the trigger and Tom fell to the floor. Will fired and the suspect fell.

'Aaagghh, my arm, you bastard, you shot me in my arm.'

Will walked over and kicked his gun away. The other hostages were frightened and had huddled together; the girls were screaming and crying.

'Tom, are you OK?' Will shouted.

'Yeah, he hit my vest,' Tom replied. 'Shit, that hurt, it's definitely going to leave a bruise.'

'My arm, I can't believe this,' cried the suspect clutching his arm.

'Lucky it wasn't your head,' Will said, standing over him.

'Just bad aim is all.'

'Bad aim?' Will looked around him. He picked up a Coke can, walked down and put it on the end of a bench, walked back and fired one shot. The can fell on the floor. Will picked it up and there was a hole right on the 'o'. 'See, I have perfect aim, if I had wanted to hit you in the head you would in fact be dead.'

'Is that supposed to impress me?' the suspect said.

'Control, we are clear, we need EMTs and PD in here for an injured suspect and to take the hostages out.'

'Received, Alpha they are on their way in.'

'My dad is going to have you for this, he's a lawyer.'

'Really, is that supposed to impress me, because I can assure you it doesn't, but make sure you tell him you are under arrest.'

'You just destroyed my future. I will never get my basketball place; I have try-outs in a month.'

'I don't think you do,' Will replied.

The PD and EMTs came in, officers started to escort the hostages out and the EMTs started to treat the suspect.

'Hey, make sure someone goes with him and reads him his rights because he is under arrest.'

'No problem, Sergeant.'

They took the suspect out and the officer read him his rights. Tom was about to leave too.

'Tom, hold still, I want to get a photo of your vest where he shot you.'

'Really?'

'Yeah, evidence.' Will took a photo with his phone. 'Now let's get Ryan out safe.'

They collected him from the classroom next door and walked him out to a waiting squad car. They put Ryan in the back.

'Don't talk to anyone at all. A lawyer will meet you at the precinct.'

'But I don't have one, they cost too much.'

'You will when you get there.'

Will shut the door and the squad car drove away. Will made a quick phone call and then turned to Tom.

'Go get yourself checked out.'

'I'm fine.'

'Come on, I want it looked at just to be sure.' They walked over to the ambulance. 'Can you check him over? He got hit in the vest but it was quite close range.'

'Yeah, sure, come on sit down. Take off your vest. Let's have a look.'

Tom took his vest off and lifted his shirt; there was a bruise already forming.

'I'm just going to check your ribs.'

'Wow, that's sore.'

'Sorry, all seems fine, nothing broken just bruised.'

Just then Richards walked over. She stared at Tom for a moment and then turned to Will.

'All packed up and ready to go, Sergeant.'

'OK, Richards, come on, Tom, let's get you back. You know that Lynne would kill me if you ever got seriously hurt. At least I can say this wasn't my fault.'

They headed back to the truck. When it was just the two of them, Will asked the question he needed an answer to.

'Did you mean what you said to Ryan in there, about rich kids and being bullied?'

'Sadly yes, until you came to my school that was my life. You changed things by being my friend. If you hadn't, I could have ended up just like Ryan.'

'Wow, I never knew that; you have never told me before.'

'It's not something I like to talk about too often.'

'Well, I'm glad you could help that kid, and hopefully the lawyer I got him will sort it all out so he can start a new school and enjoy his life again. Fresh start.'

'Yeah, that would be good.'

They got in the truck and headed back to the office.

Chapter 8

When they got back, Tom sat at his desk holding his ribs, and Will went and got them both a coffee. He walked back over, put them down and sat on Tom's desk. Bennett was holding the coke can; he had gone and collected it from the school when he was told about it. He had always been in awe of Will and his skills with a gun. He had taken a lot of criticism when he started but stuck it out in Alpha because he wanted to work with Will.

'I can't believe this; it is so cool,' turning it round and round.

'Yeah, well, the sergeant was just proving a point. Some kids today have no respect for anyone even cops.'

Bennett looked over at the two recruits sat waiting for an interview outside Kathy's office.

'So, Sergeant, how good do you think they are?'

'They must be pretty good to get to interview but they aren't as good as us,' Will replied.

'Excuse me,' one of the recruits said, 'how can you judge how good we are when you don't know us?'

Will turned around to face him.

'Really, well why don't you show us how good you are.'

'How do you expect me to do that when I'm waiting for my interview with Sergeant Hill, I can't just leave until afterwards.'

'Oh, that's simple, just a bit of fun, quick draw, see who is faster.' Will smirked.

'Seriously?'

'Yeah then if you make it onto SWAT, we can go down to the range and see who is really better.'

'OK, sure, though I'm not sure how it proves who is better.'

Will turned to Tom, smiling. He had often played these kinds of games with new recruits that came into the unit. Most of them thought they were better than everyone else but most of them were all talk. Will had discovered that it was a quick way to make them realise they had to learn and work hard to be the best.

'You say draw, OK, Tom?'

'Yeah, sure thing.'

The recruit stood up and Will stood about two feet away from him. Will smiled as they looked at each other, then Tom said, 'Draw.'

Will pulled his handgun and had it pointing at the recruit before he even had time to move.

'I guess I win,' Will said smiling.

'Sergeant Falco, will you please stop messing around with the recruits!' Captain Bridge shouted over.

Will put his gun away in its holster.

'Just having fun, Captain.'

'Yes, I see that, Sergeant, but shouldn't your team be training today and not playing games?'

'Yes, Captain, we were just getting coffee after the call is all. OK, Tom, you write up your report and relax. The rest of you let's go, there is circuit training to be done.'

Kathy came to get the recruit for interview just as everyone was leaving, laughing and chatting as they went. She looked around, wondering what had been going on. She gestured to the recruit to come in and he went into her office. She grabbed another cup of coffee and went in closing the door behind her.

***

After an hour Kathy had finished with the interviews and she came out for another coffee. The interviews had taken their toll on her, that was for sure. Her leg was aching even though she had been sat most of the day; maybe that was the problem. Tom was getting one, and she could see he was obviously in pain.

'What happened to you?'

'Took one close range in the vest, just a bit bruised.'

'Do you want me to have a look?'

'No, I'm OK, EMTs said it's just a bad bruise.'

'I have something that will help with that.' She disappeared into her office and came back out with a tube of gel.

'This stuff is amazing, trust me, come on, sit down.'

Tom sat on the chair and lifted his shirt.

'Wow, that's bad, are you sure you didn't break a rib or something?'

'EMT said not, it was close range though. Had this a few years back, but that was in the back.'

Kathy was rubbing some gel into the bruise when Tom suddenly pulled his shirt down and stood up. Kathy turned around to see Will. She stood up. Will said nothing and went into his office, Tom followed.

'That wasn't…'

'Yeah, I know,' Will said as he looked through a filing cabinet.

'Good because I would hate you to think something was going on. She was just putting something on my ribs.'

'OK.' He pulled out some papers and looked at Tom. I know you wouldn't cheat on Lynne so I don't see what the issue is.'

'Because it's Kathy.'

'She's single, she can touch who she likes.'

'But I know you wanted to sort things out.'

'Well, she decided that the truth means we can't be together, which confused the hell out of me. I would have told you earlier but we got busy and I didn't manage to speak to you without the others being there.'

Will walked out of his office and was heading towards the office door to go back downstairs when Kathy stopped him.

'Can I have a word please, Sergeant?'

'I'm a bit busy with circuit training but I can spare five minutes.'

They went in her office and he shut the door. He stood by the door and she moved behind her desk.

'Do you want to tell me what happened earlier with Officer Stanson?'

'Who?'

'Well, he was my best option, but now he isn't sure he wants to join after having a gun pointed at him.'

'Then he's going for the wrong job.'

'He meant by you,' she almost shouted.

'Seriously, that was just a bit of fun.'

'For who?'

'OK, so he may not have found it fun, but he didn't have to agree to play either, no big deal,' Will said folding his arms.

'Well, it is if I lose him from my team.'

'If he can't take a joke maybe he isn't the best fit.'

'That's not your call.'

'But he will be working with my team, watching our backs.'

'Still not your call.'

'What's the real issue here, Kathy? Me, I am guessing.'

Kathy didn't answer; she looked away.

'You said you didn't want me, yet you are angry with me. I never did anything.'

'You lied,' she said, turning back to face him.

'No, I didn't tell you because I knew it would be an issue,' he shouted.

'You never gave me a chance.'

'And yet you proved me right anyway, so I guess I was right all along.'

Will stepped towards the door.

'You are angry, fine, but if we can't work together and the captain moves one of us, who do you think that will be, Kathy?' He paused. 'I am willing to work with you if you can get over yourself and move on, because this was your decision and not mine.'

'Wow, could your ego possibly get any bigger?'

'This isn't about me; you need to decide what you want to do, work with me or not, it's your choice but don't get mad with me if you get put on nights.' He opened the door. 'Now, if you're done, I have work to do.'

He walked out of the office, furious. Tom went over to Kathy.

'Kathy, you know I love you, but don't go head to head with him. There will only ever be one loser and it won't be Will.'

Deep down she knew he was right so she had to try and handle this before he did.

Chapter 9

Next morning Will came into the office and he could see Kathy in with the captain. He poured a coffee and headed towards his own when the captain came to his door.

'Sergeant Falco, can you join us please.'

Will followed the captain in. Kathy was sat down. Will shut the door and stood by it.

'Now, I understand we have some issues with you two getting along due to personal differences. The introduction of a new team was intended to work alongside Alpha team, but I have been told by Sergeant Hill this morning that this may be an issue now.'

'I have no problem, Captain,' Will replied. 'I know Sergeant Hill is a good officer and I will happily work with her and her team.'

'I have an issue,' answered Kathy. 'Sergeant Falco has a need to be better than anyone else, playing games and pulling stunts with my recruits to the point where they are questioning joining the unit.'

'That was a joke, and he did actually agree to playing the game. No one forced him. Ask any of my team.'

'No one but you and your team found it funny, even the other recruit asked if it was normal for those things to happen.'

'Now you two, this has to stop.' The captain stood and looked out of the window behind his desk. 'Fact is, Sergeant Hill, Alpha team will stay as they are, they are my best team. Sergeant Falco is my best officer and team leader, and I need them on my busiest shifts, but I want you to run Bravo team. However, if you can't then I will have to put your team on nights, which I would rather avoid doing but I can't have two teams on days that can't work together.'

'Yes, Captain' said Kathy sadly. She had been hoping by going to the captain first he would have had a better answer for her.

'Now, can you leave me and Sergeant Falco to have a chat.'

Kathy got up and left closing the door as she went.

'Now, Sergeant Falco, you may be my Alpha team but you need to find a way to make it right with Sergeant Hill. She is an excellent officer and it would be a massive loss if I had to put her on a different shift. If you can't sort this, Alpha may find the odd graveyard shift on their rota. Do I make myself clear?'

'Yes, Captain,' Will replied, 'I will do my best.'

Will left his office and walked straight into his own. He didn't think that Kathy would be so upset over this and he knew it had more to do with them than him messing around with her recruit. He knew it was a low move but he was all over the place and the recruit had annoyed him. It had taken Will years to get his team as good as they were and he wasn't going to let a recruit think he could match up. Tom knocked on his door.

'What was that about?'

'Kathy complained to the captain about yesterday, said she couldn't work with me.'

'What? What did the captain say?'

'That we needed to work it out or she would be on permanent nights and we would be on the odd shit shift.'

'Oh, so now what?'

'I don't know. She made this decision. I'm the one that should be mad about it but she is so angry with me, I reckon if I give her enough space, she may be OK to the point we can work together at least.'

'OK, if you need me to help with anything just shout because I like the shifts we have just fine.'

The rest of the day was a busy one, constant call outs, and Will was looking forward to having a second team to pick up some of the calls because it seemed it was getting busier of late, and Alpha were run right to their limit most days, and he was struggling to keep up with training and all the paper work.

**

That evening as Will was finishing his paperwork for the day the captain appeared at his door.

'Sergeant Falco, I have the ADA in my office and she needs to speak with you.'

'OK.' Will got up and followed the captain into his office.

The captain shut the door behind them and went and sat behind his desk. There was a woman sitting opposite him; she turned to look at Will and smiled.

'Sergeant Falco, we have some news for you over Mr X.'

The man who had killed Will's parents could only be referred to in that way because he refused to give his name and had never been in any system.

'OK, what's that?'

'He has agreed to plead guilty on all charges and serve the full life sentence, but there is one condition.'

'And what is that condition?'

'You go and speak with him for an hour and answer whatever questions he asks you.'

'And why the hell would I do that?'

'He says if you don't agree he will take the stand at trial and tell the court and everyone there exactly who you are and what you did for him at the bank. Now, I am thinking he will exaggerate it all considerably. I asked the judge if we could have a closed court for the case as some information that could be disclosed was sensitive and it was declined. So, I am here seeing what you want to do.'

Will stood for a few moments in silence. He wasn't sure what this guy was going to get out of speaking with him and what twisted game he was trying to play, but the alternative could destroy him and the unit.

'OK, I will go and speak with him.'

'You are sure, Sergeant?' Captain Bridge asked him.

'Do I really have much choice? Either I do or he brings me and this whole unit down. I can't allow that to happen, and if it means no trial is that not better anyway if he doesn't want anything else?'

'OK, when do you want to go, and I will sort it out?'

'Tomorrow morning, first thing, get it over and done with.'

'OK, Sergeant, I will get the papers drawn up and signed and will get you in to see him; just be careful, we don't know why he wants this meet.'

'I'm pretty sure it's to play games with my head, but I will be careful.'

Will left and went back in his office. He saw Kathy head towards the captain's office. He knew she would be happy at not having to go to trial at least. About fifteen minutes later Kathy stood at his office door.

'Can I help you with something, Sergeant Hill?' he asked without looking up.

'They told me about the deal.'

'I presumed they would, now there won't be a trial,' he replied, putting his pen down and looking at her.

'You are really going to see him? After everything he has done?'

'Yes, because it's the best option.'

'If it's on my account you don't have to. I was ready for the trial.'

'Actually, my decision was not based around you at all. It's my decision, Sergeant. The ADA set out the options available and I chose. I didn't realise I had to run my decisions by you,' he said sarcastically. 'Now is that all because I have an early start at the prison?'

'Just because I am angry with you right now doesn't mean I don't care about you, Will, and I don't want him messing with your head, that's all.'

Will grabbed his stuff and stopped in front of her at the door. She stepped aside and, as he passed, he paused.

'But you chose not to be with me, Kathy, so it's got nothing to do with you now, does it? Now I need to get home.'

He walked off and Kathy was standing fighting the tears back. She did care for him and still loved him and that hurt her more than she liked to admit.

Chapter 10

The next morning Will had got to the prison for eight o'clock. He didn't want it to cut into his shift too much because without Richards on the team, it was already tough enough. He had called Tom and told him he would be later in and said to get dispatch to put them on emergencies till he got in. He went through all the security check points and had left his helmet with the guards as he went in. He went into a room and then two guards brought him in and handcuffed him to the table. Will was standing by the wall as they did so. Watching in silence, he got some satisfaction at seeing him like this. After the guards had gone, he spoke.

'Sergeant Falco, how nice of you to agree to see me, even if it took a deal to get you here.'

'Yeah, I think I'm missing what is in this for you.' He sat down opposite him.

'I get to speak with you. I knew you wouldn't come if I just asked.'

'You're right there, so shall we get on with this so I can get to work.'

'Yes, of course, busy, are we?'

'Yeah, it has been.'

'Is Kathy back at work yet?'

'Yes, she is, but just in the office.'

'Really, didn't take her for a desk type of person.'

'She is training a new team. She's a sergeant now and she hasn't been cleared for full duty yet, thanks to you.'

'Yes, it was one of my more regrettable actions. I do actually like her: she is feisty.'

Will looked at him in a way he picked up on.

'You have split up.'

'What makes you say that?'

'I can tell by your face when I talk about her, too many secrets, Sergeant.'

'She knows everything, but yeah, we split up.'

'After all you did for her, saving her life and all. She doesn't love you as much as you thought perhaps and I know you didn't tell her everything, did you? I know you, Sergeant. Hardly anyone knows who you are or what happened in your past.'

'You know but you keep quiet.'

'Yes, because it serves my purpose and, Sergeant, I may have had to kill your parents but I respect you. You are very good at what you do, so dedicated to your job, very admirable.'

They sat for a moment observing each other. Will knew he was a very intelligent man and he knew not to underestimate him at all. He also knew he had to answer his questions.

'So, Sergeant, are you going to fight for the lovely Kathy, or are you going to let the best one you've had get away?'

'It's not up to me, it's up to her.'

'Yes, in part but I always thought you as a man who would stand up and fight for what he wanted, not hide away in a corner.'

'I'm not hiding, I am giving her space.'

'Her or you? You don't let anyone get too close, do you? She hasn't been to your place yet, didn't know who you are. Just how did you last so long with all those secrets?'

'Love, because we still have that even if she is mad.'

He smiled at Will for a moment.

'So how is Ashleigh? I loved her last movie. She hasn't been around much of late but I guess that's her job.'

'She's good, but...'

'I know everything about you, Sergeant, so don't be so surprised by things like that. We aren't that different you know, Sergeant.'

'How so?'

'Both intelligent, have killed people, work hard.'

'I haven't murdered anyone.'

'They only don't call it murder because you have a badge, and that is supposed to make it OK.'

'I save innocent people, and not that it matters to you but I don't enjoy killing people. I only do it when I have to.'

'I don't enjoy it, Sergeant. I don't really feel anything any more. You see, the first person I killed was my wife. The one person I had ever loved in this world. My parents didn't want me. I never had any friends really all through my education. I met my wife and she adored me; we were so happy. Then I caught her in bed with my next-door neighbour. So, I killed them both while they were in our bed. After that is was easy to kill anyone else, because I was numb from all emotion. I still am really, but don't feel sorry for me because I enjoyed the challenge of being ahead of you and the police. It was quite fun.'

'I don't feel sorry for you. You murdered so many people that I never will. It's a bit of a cliché though right, killing your wife for cheating and then her lover, and now you are too cold and just kill anyone.'

'A cliché? Sergeant, I am definitely not that.'

'See I'm not so sure. Did you kill your parents for not loving you too?'

'I believe I am supposed to be asking the questions, Sergeant.'

'That's a yes then, see, just a cliché.'

'OK, enough, Sergeant, or you won't find out why I wanted to speak to you.'

'I thought it was to catch up and ask me questions.'

'In part yes, but you caught me when no one else could and now I feel that I owe you a prize of some sort.'

'What do you mean a prize?'

'Nothing sinister, Sergeant, don't worry.'

'That remains to be seen.'

'Now, Sergeant, that's no way to be. I am here trying to help you out and asking for nothing in return.'

'Nothing? I am not here for nothing, am I?'

'Sergeant, you are here because you didn't want Kathy to have to go through a trial. You are scared I will expose your secrets, and tell them everything I know.'

'Well, I don't make a habit of meeting with criminals like you, so are you going to tell me what this supposed prize is?'

'OK, Sergeant, you have earned it. Even though I am in here I still have many people on the outside and I hear things. I will not give you or anyone else any more so here it is: you need to watch your back, Sergeant, because someone is coming after you.'

'What?'

'You heard me, Sergeant, a onetime tip, and believe me, you wouldn't have seen it coming otherwise.'

'How do you know this?'

'Like I say I have my contacts.'

'But to know someone is after me.'

'They are very good at what they do, Sergeant. It isn't just one, I have many people willing to tell me things.'

'But to know this is different; you must know who it is.'

'Maybe I do but I think you have had enough information from me now.'

'You haven't given me anything.'

'Whether you know it or not I may have just saved your life, Sergeant, and I really don't make a habit of those kind of things, it's not good for my image. I didn't have to tell you but you getting killed is no good from my perspective, so yes, it's perhaps a selfish warning but take it because it's the only one you will get. Well, goodbye, Sergeant, it's been fun. Guards I'm finished.'

The guards came in and took him out, and all Will could do was sit there and watch him go, wondering what he meant.

When Will got back to the office, his team were sitting at their desks, talking. He got a coffee and went straight to his office. Tom followed him and shut the door. Will sat down and Tom stood by the door.

'So, what happened?'

'Not much, he asked about Kathy and Ash, and then he told me that someone was coming after me, wouldn't say any more but apparently the tip was my prize for catching him, said I wouldn't see it coming if he hadn't told me.'

'Is he just messing with you?'

'I don't know, so keep it to yourself in case he is. We know he likes to play mind games, but at least it means there won't be a trial now, so let's get some work done.'

Tom left the office and Kathy walked past. She paused and was going to ask how it went but thought better of it. Will watched her. He needed to stay away from her for a while and see what happened.

***

Over the next two weeks, Will took every call possible and was out of the office a lot to avoid Kathy. He thought if he gave her enough space then she would be able to start moving on and perhaps they would be able to work together, if she could just get over the anger. He went on a couple of dates, but he wasn't really interested. It was more to get him out and stop him thinking about her. He was well and truly in love with Kathy, and it was going to take him a long time to get over it, but he tried to be as professional as possible when they crossed paths.

Thursdays were usually quiet so he grabbed his usual morning coffee and went into his office to get some paperwork done. It was the ball this weekend so he wanted to make sure he was all clear for the Saturday to allow him and the team to be off. He had just sat down when the captain appeared at his door.

'Sergeant, I need your help today. You see, I have a problem. Sergeant Hill's recruits are not making any progress on the range, so I need you to go down there and help out today.'

'Sergeant Hill agreed to that?'

'She doesn't have to, it's an order from me to you.'

'Yes, Captain, I will be right on it after my coffee.'

'Be on the range by eight thirty. I want these recruits sorted out. I don't want them to fail and they are fast running out of time. If they do, it will look bad on this unit and on Sergeant Hill and could very well affect her future.'

Captain Bridge went back to his office. Will sat back in his chair and drank his coffee. He knew she wouldn't be happy with him helping but he knew that she should be well on top of their training; she was a very talented officer. She may not like it but he needed to help sort these recruits and find out why she was not making progress with them.

***

Will walked onto the range just before eight thirty. Kathy was already there with her team and they were just getting set up. She saw him and walked straight over.

'Sergeant, I have the range booked all day.'

'I know, the captain sent me down to help.'

'Seriously?'

'Yeah, he thought you could use an extra pair of hands, that's all.'

'Fine, you take Ford, Blain and Fremont,' she said, pointing to the three closest to Will, 'and I will take the others.'

'OK, sure thing.'

Kathy walked away and started working with the officer furthest away. Will walked over to Ford.

'OK, let's see what you have got.'

Ford took up his aim position and was about to fire when Will stopped him.

'Wait, that's not quite right, all three of you watch me for a moment.'

Will stood and aimed down the range.

'Now, do you all see the difference?'

All three of them nodded and copied how Will had been standing. He checked each one of them before he allowed them to fire a shot.

'Better, soften your knees a little and relax. If you tense your shot will be off where you are aiming.'

'Yes, Sergeant,' Ford replied.

All three of them fired their clips and put their weapons down. Will brought the three targets forward and looked at them.

'These are all pretty good. You are not far off where you need to be, try again.'

Will looked over to Kathy and realised she wasn't wearing her handguns. He turned to Ford.

'Hasn't Sergeant Hill showed you all this already?'

'Not really, she positions us but never shows us.'

'Really, she's an awesome shot and one hell of a SWAT officer.' He paused and thought for a moment. 'You three carry on with what I just showed you, and I will be back in ten.'

Will came back fifteen minutes later; the three officers were getting better with each clip of rounds. Will retrieved their last targets and was looking at them.

'These are much better, you see, you have been able to bring the strays more into the centre. They are the ones you need to get rid of. You can't have stray bullets when you are on a call.'

They went back to their booths, and Blain aimed down the range once more.

'Wait a second.' Will stopped him. 'When you are aiming,' he pulled his handgun again, 'bring your gun up, don't use your neck to aim too much. You need to limit how much strain you put on your neck because on calls when you are in a standoff you are going to feel it, believe me. Now with your main weapon you will bring your head down to aim but don't hold like that. You will learn how to work so you are comfortable. You need to keep your arms bent and relaxed so you have movement to re-aim if someone moves.'

'What's the red for, Sergeant?' Blain asked, indicating to his tape on the trigger guard.

'It's my call sign. Alpha team all have a colour and each of my weapons has red on them.'

'Will we use that too?'

'I don't know, that's up to Sergeant Hill. Other teams use numbers, I like colours.'

Will looked at the time. He went over to Kathy and suggested a break. As the others left, he stopped Kathy.

'Can I borrow you for a minute, Sergeant?'
'What for?'

Will allowed the others to leave before he said any more. Then he put Kathy's handgun on the top at one of the range booths.

'Imagine my surprise when Wayne told me you hadn't signed your weapons out since you came back, not even for training.'

'I don't need them.'

'Really, you don't, showing your team is better than explaining, you know that.'

'I choose to do it differently.'

'And you do realise when on duty you should at least carry your handguns.'

'Yeah, well, being in the office, I haven't exactly needed them.'

'Come on, Kathy.'

'Come one what? I don't know what you are trying to insinuate, Will, but it's wrong,' she said, even more defiantly

'OK, if I'm wrong take your gun and fire it at the target.'

'Fine, I will.'

She picked up her gun that Will had put there and aimed. She took a deep breath but then started shaking and put it down. She put her head down and then turned to Will.

'You happy now.'

'No, of course not, why would I be?' He turned her back round to face the target. 'Now pick up your weapon, and close your eyes, think only of the target and breathe. Now focus.' He moved closer behind her. 'Now open your eyes and aim.'

She aimed but her hands started to shake again. He put his arms around her and supported them.

'Now pull the trigger.'

She fired, again and again till the clip was empty. Will retrieved the target; it was near perfect. She turned around to face him, only coming to his chest. She looked up.

'Thanks, Will.'

'My pleasure.'

They were so close in that moment she could feel him breathing; the moment was so intense. She suddenly pulled his face towards hers and kissed him. Then stopped.

'Sorry, I shouldn't have done that.'

'Never be sorry for doing that.'

He leaned forward and kissed her, lovingly and softly.

Just then his beeper went off.

'Damn it, that's bad timing.'

'Just a little.'

'I will be back later, hopefully.'

He touched her cheek gently and then kissed her again before flashing her a smile and then left. Kathy reloaded and fired another clip. She suddenly felt whole again, a feeling she hadn't had since she was shot.

Chapter 11

It was the end of shift when the team finally walked back in the office. There had been two call outs that amounted to nothing.

'I can't believe they had us sat on the roof for hours and then they had gone out the back, and the other was just as bad. What a boring shift,' Tom complained as he got coffee.

'I know but what can we do?' replied Will.

'OK, who are you and what did you do with Sergeant Falco.'

'Very funny, I have been ordered to play nice remember.'

'Ah, yes of course, but you don't usually actually do that.'

'Well, as there are no reports to write for our efforts, I'm going. Enjoy your evenings.'

With that Will left the office.

'Well that's different,' Harvey commented.

'How so?' Richards asked.

'He's never that happy, but then he did spend a few hours of this morning down on the range with a certain sergeant. I wonder if anything happened?' Harvey replied.

'Well, let's hope so because he's much easier to work with,' Bennett chipped in.

Richards pulled her phone out and sent a text. *Meet me in thirty mins, we are going to have to think of something else as this just isn't working.*

***

Will rode to Kathy's house. He needed to know if there was more to the kiss, possibly a sign that they could be moving forward and there was a chance to get back together. Will bounced up the steps to Kathy's front door. He knocked but when the door opened, to his shock, it was Officer Stanson standing in front of him. He was five foot eleven, with brown hair but fair skin. He was a similar build to Will and obviously kept in shape.

'Is Sergeant Hill around?' Will asked.

'Kathy, someone here for you,' he called back towards the living room.

Kathy appeared in her dressing gown.

'Oh hi, I wasn't expecting you tonight.'

'So, it seems.' He took a step back. 'Listen, I should go.'

Will walked back down the steps, somewhat deflated. He got on his motorcycle and rode off.

'Damn it,' Kathy said closing the door.

She headed back into the living room. Her new team were all there along with Gina. They were trying on outfits for Saturday's police ball. Gina knew someone who worked at a designer store and so had arranged the evening, though she wouldn't be there as it was her mother's birthday party on the same evening. She knew it was important to Kathy.

'Pass me a glass of wine,' Kathy said to Gina.

'I thought you weren't drinking because of your painkillers.'

'Well, that was Will at the door and I'm pretty sure he now thinks I am sleeping with Stanson over there, so I need a drink.'

'Shit, really? Well you need to fix this and quick because a man like that won't wait around forever.'

'I know, I will speak to him in the morning, and if all else fails I will see him at the ball, so I need the best dress they have.'

***

Next morning Kathy went into the office. Tom was in early sat with a cup of coffee. Kathy looked into Will's office, but he wasn't there.

'Is Will not in yet?'

'No, he's in court this morning, that shopping mall thing that Richards caused. The parents are suing and want to get a reason for criminal charges to be brought up against the unit.'

'Oh, shit, that's not good. Will he be in later?'

'Possibly, I don't know yet.'

'Right, well, I'm out training for the day. I may catch him later.'

She left the office and sent Will a text saying they needed to talk.

***

Will was sitting in court an hour before he was called in. He was sworn in and the lawyer for the families started his questions.

'Sergeant Falco, you and your team carried out an offensive that took the lives of three males in a shopping mall just outside the city, didn't you?'

'Yes.'

'It was one of your officers that fired which caused the boys to react?'

'Yes.'

'Was that officer authorised to fire?'

'No.'

'Did the officer get reprimanded?'

'Yes.'

'For what exactly?'

'For disobeying the hold.'

'And?'

'For missing.'

'So, the officer was disciplined for not hitting the boys.'

'Yes.'

'And why was that?'

'I run the Alpha team and we don't miss, and if the officer hadn't missed, they wouldn't have fired at my team.'

'In fact, Sergeant, you and your team have the highest number of fatal shootings in the whole of the police department, don't you?'

'Yes, because we have more call outs to shootings and hostage situations.'

'But did you need to kill the boys in this case?'

'I don't kill anyone, unless I don't have another choice.'

'Really, including these three boys, you kill them and that's OK.'

'I was doing my job.'

'Yes, well it must come easy to you to take such young lives. No further questions.'

The lawyer for the Police Department had no questions, so Will stepped down and left the court room. The parents followed him out.

'Sergeant!' one of the mothers shouted.

Will stopped and turned around. He hated dealing with the families of the suspects under usual circumstances. He never needed to, but he always hated this part of the job: explaining why he did what he did was never easy for him.

'How can you be so cold and callous? They were our sons that you and your team killed.'

'I was doing my job.'

'How can you sleep at night? You make a choice to kill people.'

Will stepped towards her.

'It's never my choice. Your sons chose to enter that mall with guns; they chose to shoot and injure people as they went in; they chose to hold over one hundred people hostage and they chose to shoot at me and my team. They weren't forced and when they did all those things, they left me with no choice. I never go to any call with the purpose of killing anyone, but if that's the only choice I'm left with then it's the only one I can make.'

Will's beeper went off; he had switched it back on as he left the court room. He took out his phone and called Tom.

'What we got?' He moved away from the parents. 'OK, grab my gear I will meet you there.' He turned back to them. 'Excuse me, I have work to do.' He walked off leaving the parents to consider what he had said.

***

Will pulled up outside the hotel and as he did so Tom and his team arrived in the truck. Will got his gear out and suited up before heading over to Lieutenant Planter who was standing with Sergeant Dune. Dune didn't like Will and he had been the one who had arrested him after he robbed a bank to save Kathy.

'OK, Sergeant Falco, we have an armed suspect in the reception. He won't talk to us. He hasn't shot anyone yet but he is waving a gun around at the staff that are at the reception desk.'

'So how are we going in?' Will asked.

'Through the kitchen at the back and up the stairs to the reception area. When in, Delta team will go in through the front doors and head towards the reception area.'

'So, both teams are going in?'

'Yes, but, Sergeant Falco, you have point on this as always.'

Lieutenant Planter walked away back to the incident truck.

'Think you can handle that, Dune, me being in charge?'

'You do your job, Falco, and I will do mine. Just don't do anything reckless or stupid like you usually do.'

Will's team went through the kitchen at the back of the hotel. They went up the stairs slowly. They came out behind the elevators. They moved slowly till Will was level with the end. Will could see the suspect; he was agitated, pacing up and down. Will didn't want to overwhelm him, so he signalled to the team to hold where they were. He was going to go it alone on this one.

'Control, this is Alpha team, we are in position. Hold Delta team outside till my signal. The suspect seems agitated and anxious so we don't need to many officers in here; it may make him fire.'

'Received, Alpha team.'

Will slowly stepped forward. The suspect spun round and saw him.

'What are you doing? Who are you?'

'I'm Sergeant Falco from NYPD. I'm here to help you. Can you tell me what the problem is?'

'They,' he said pointing to the receptionist, 'are recording me and they won't stop.'

'OK.' Will lowered his weapon slightly. 'Do you mean the CCTV?'

'No, they are recording me in my room too, and they won't stop.'

'If I get them to stop, can you put the gun down?'

'Yes,' he smiled, 'but they will tell me if it's stopped.'

'Who will tell you?'

'Them,' he said, tapping his head.

Will walked towards him slowly. He got to the reception desk and stopped two feet away.

'Can you turn off all the surveillance everywhere, please,' Will said to the receptionist.

'Yes, but…'

Will put his hand up to stop her.

'Just turn them ALL off.'

'OK,' she said and proceeded to turn them all off.

'OK they are all off.'

'Thank you very much.' He started to hand his gun to Will when a shot rang out; the suspect dropped to the floor dead. Will turned to see Sergeant Dune lowering his weapon, smiling.

'What the fuck was that, Dune?' Will shouted

'My job, of course.'

'He wasn't a threat; he was giving me his gun.'

'Oh well, my mistake,' he said and then he turned and walked off.

Will signalled to his team and headed out.

'This is not over,' Will said to Tom.

***

They got back to the office and Sergeant Dune was sitting with his team laughing. Will walked straight past them and into the captain's office, closing the door. Twenty minutes later a lieutenant appeared with two detectives; they were from internal affairs, and they went into the captain's office, and then five minutes later they came back out and walked over to Dune. He stood up and looked at them.

'Can I help you guys with something?'

'Sergeant Dune you are under arrest.'

'What for?'

'Unlawful killing.'

Sergeant Dune turned to see Will standing, arms folded, outside the captain's office; he was looking straight at Dune.

'You bastard, you did this.'

Will stayed silent.

'After all the crap you get away with in this unit, the arguments, threatening officers, robbing a fucking bank, and you have me arrested. This is because I arrested you, isn't it? Is it meant to be payback?'

'No, you shot and killed a man that was mentally ill and not a threat, that was handing his gun to me, and all you can say is "oh well, my mistake". This is not payback, it's justice.'

The detectives walked Dune out. Captain Bridge signalled Dune's team into his office. Will went and got a coffee.

'Good call, Sergeant,' Harvey said.

Will nodded and headed back into his office, closing the door.

Chapter 12

Will sat at his desk with a coffee. He had never done what he just did before. He hated it even though he knew it was the right thing to do, though, thinking about it, he had never needed to. In all his years on SWAT and the force, there had been very few officers that had killed a person in the way that Dune just had. Will had always done his best to talk someone down and had only fired first without speaking, if he was fired upon first. He thought about what Dune had said to him. Had he got away with that much aside from the bank robbery? Most of his reprimands were on the back of falling out with the PD, not for a bad shoot, but now he was going over so many in his head. Shoots had gone bad, like the one with his parents, but he hadn't pulled the trigger and he had never hit a hostage in all his years on SWAT. He had never crossed the line that Dune did today; he was sure he hadn't. He only knew of two others that had in the whole of the unit and they were no longer serving. He looked at his phone. There were three texts from Kathy asking to talk. He couldn't deal with that right now; he just needed a drink and some sleep. The summer ball was tomorrow and he wanted to be at the venue most of the day for the set up.

***

Kathy was packing up for the day at the training area just outside the city. It had buildings, assault courses and ranges to test all teams to the full. She looked at her phone. She had texted Will three times and he still hadn't answered. He must be still mad at her. She put her phone away as Stanson walked over.

'You deserve better you know, Sergeant.'

'I'm sorry.'

'You deserve better than Sergeant Falco. You should be with someone who treats you right.'

'Well, Stanson, it's really none of your business, and Sergeant Falco is a good man.' She paused and looked at Stanson. 'I will see you tomorrow. We are meeting at mine and all going to the ball together.'

'Yeah, OK, I will see you tomorrow.'

He walked away and Kathy finished getting everything into the car. She just wanted to get back and unload the stuff, so she could get home and have a soak in the bath.

***

The summer ball was the highlight of the year for so many police officers in the NYPD. Not everyone could attend, of course, and many departments put their officers on a rota to go. Will had redesigned the ball when his parents died, when he started paying for it. It was a busy time: he had to choose menus and music and find out who was going to enable the seating to be organised. He always put departments near him that he got on with as he never wanted any issue on this evening and wanted everyone to get along. Every department agreed, though, that the ball was better than ever. Will ensured his team didn't work that Saturday in trade for an on-call shift on the Sunday, so they couldn't drink but that had never bothered his team. For the first time in many years, he didn't have a date tonight. Even if Kathy had moved on, he hadn't.

Will was sitting at the bar when everyone started to arrive at the ball. It was held at a spa hotel and had been for the past five years; Will knew the managers and so it had been easy to arrange. It had a very large function room with a dance floor. It was often used for weddings but it was perfect for the ball. The only people that knew he paid for it all was Tom, the captain and the chief. The senior officers had their own tables and tended to leave straight after the meal and very rarely spoke to the lower-ranking officers, as was usual, especially outside of the office.

'Hey, Will, you have scrubbed up well as always.' Will turned around to see Tom and Lynne.

'Thanks, Lynne, you look stunning.'

Lynne was Tom's wife. She was nearly as tall as Tom with long blonde hair. She had a beautiful evening gown on, emerald green in colour with V-neck and a low back. She always looked elegant even when she had a pair of jeans on. She leaned forward for a hug and kissed Will on the cheek.

'So, no date tonight?'

'No not tonight.'

'Really, why's that?'

'Will is hoping to win back the lovely Kathy, aren't you, buddy?'

'Well that depends on Kathy.'

'Sweetheart, you know any woman would be lucky to have you,' Lynne stated.

Just then Richards, Bennett and Palmer arrived.

'Hey, everyone, looking good, Sergeant,' Richards said eagerly.

Will looked at her. She had a full-length dress on in white. It left little to the imagination; it was cut to expose her sides down to her hips, and had a split up the side well up her thigh. It was far too tight for her size, and Will definitely didn't approve of it and he turned away, without responding to her.

'What table are we at, Sergeant?' asked Bennett.

'Table one, of course.'

Bennett and Palmer went over to the table to find their seats then went and grabbed a drink from the bar.

'So, Sergeant, do I get a dance later?' Richards said flirtatiously, trying to regain his attention.

'I don't dance,' Will replied as he stood. He then walked off towards the table, followed by Lynne and Tom.

Richards stood at the bar for a moment, furious. What did she have to do to get this guy to notice her? She ordered a whiskey from the bar and downed it in one drink. She headed over to the table and found she was at the opposite side of the table to Will; she was about to say something when Harvey and Selena arrived. Will stood and greeted them, kissing Selena on the cheek.

'Wow, Selena, you look amazing; I am so jealous right now.'

Selena was African American, like her husband, Dan Harvey. She was very curvaceous, with long black hair. She had on a sparkling blue dress with diamante on the thin straps and across the top. She, like Lynne, was always elegant and Will saw how lucky his friends were to have such amazing women by their sides. He had decided he wanted that and Kathy was the one for him.

'Will, thank you. You look so handsome tonight. Dan tells me you have turned over a new leaf and only have eyes for one woman.'

'He's right. No more playing around for me. I only have eyes for Kathy.'

'That's so lovely to hear,' Selena said, giving him a hug.

Richards was in a stall in the ladies' room, working out her next move. She heard two women come in; she stayed quiet and listened to their conversation.

'So, Tom was telling me that new one, Richards, has got such a crush on Will.'

'She doesn't stand a chance. You heard what he said, only has eyes for Kathy.'

'Yeah, I'm so happy he has finally found one he wants for good and besides, did you see Richards? That dress looks awful, absolutely no class at all. Tom said Will can't stand her and doesn't trust her at all. He is apparently getting rid of her.'

'And we all know Will always gets what he wants.'

Richards heard them leave. She knew it was Lynne and Selena. She sent a text.

We are going to bring down the whole of Alpha team starting with Sergeant Falco!

Back out in the ballroom, Will was talking to Tom when Kathy arrived. She walked in arm in arm with Stanson. She looked amazing in a stunning red gown that hugged her perfect curves, with diamante sparkling across the top. It was strapless and the top had the appearance of a love heart. She had her hair up, but with some curls down and around her face, pure class. Will got up and greeted her.

'Wow, you look amazing.'

'Thanks, you look pretty good too.'

They sat down. Will had ensured that Kathy was seated next to him, but as the meal went on, her focus was elsewhere, having conversations with nearly everyone there. Will watched her and knew that this was the woman he wanted for life.

After the four courses the band started to play and people got up to dance. Will was about to ask Kathy but

Stanson beat him to it. Will watched them dance, his hand getting lower on her back, smiling at each other, wondering if he had lost her. He got up and walked towards the door; he needed some air. The dance finished. Lynne and Selena walked to the dance floor and whisked Kathy off to the ladies' room.

'What's going on?' Kathy asked.

'An intervention,' Selena answered.

'Now, we know that you and Will have been going through a rough spell, but you need to open your eyes,' Lynne continued.

'That young thing you were dancing with may be good for fun but in the long run that won't work out,' Selena added.

'I know,' Kathy said, 'it was just a dance. I love Will and I am going to make it up to him tonight. That's why I'm wearing this, cost an absolute fortune but hopefully it will be worth it.'

Selena and Lynne looked at each other and then at Kathy, smiling.

'Well you do realise, this is the first ball in five years that he hasn't brought a date to, and he has been watching you all night. So, I think you have this in the bag.'

'Now go find him.'

Kathy walked back into the ballroom, but she couldn't see Will anywhere. She headed over to Tom.

'Tom, have you seen Will?'

'He went outside, through the door over there.'

Kathy walked slowly towards the door; she wasn't used to wearing such high heels. She heard a bang as she got to the door. She opened it slowly. Will was standing there, rubbing his hand.

'Do you want me to come back?'

Will turned to look at her, a little surprised to see her there.

'No, actually I wanted to talk to you.'

'What did you do to your hand?'

'Nothing, it's fine.'

'You sure, it looks sore.'

'I've had worse.'

'You hit the door, didn't you?'

'Yeah, I was just a bit mad with myself, and seeing you with Stanson, but I'm OK now.'

Kathy walked towards the railings and looked out at the view: beautiful gardens lit by so many lights. Will came and stood next to her.

'I came out to tell you that I made a mistake the other week and if you still want me, I want to try again.'

'Really?' Will smiled. 'I thought after the other night and you dancing with Stanson I had missed my chance.'

'Yeah really, the other night when you came around, the whole team and Gina were there. We were trying on outfits for tonight.'

'Wow, I feel stupid.'

Will put his arm around her. She turned to look at him. He kissed her softly and slowly. All Kathy wanted to do was to take him home. They stood for a while just enjoying the view, happy in the moment. Kathy felt safe with Will's arms wrapped around her. After a while she turned, looked at him and smiled.

'So how about a dance?'

'I don't dance.'

'Not even for me?'

'OK, but just one.' He smiled.

They went back inside and headed to the dance floor; the band was playing a slow number. Tom and Lynne were already dancing, and Harvey and Selena followed. Will though was lost in the moment, looking at Kathy. Then he kissed her there in front of everyone. For the first time, he didn't care who saw. After the dance they walked over to the bar and sat down. Kathy looked at Will and smiled, and Will smiled back, taking her hand and holding it, just looking into her eyes. For that moment Kathy had never been so happy. She knew it wasn't going to be easy after all that had happened but she wanted this to work more than anything.

People had started to leave as it was starting to get late. Richards was sitting at the end of the bar, extremely intoxicated. Will went to speak to Tom as he was about to leave. Richards approached Kathy.

'You don't deserve a man like that and you won't keep him. He will see you for what you really are soon enough, a gold digger.'

'What?' Kathy was shocked. 'You know how much sergeants get paid; there is no gold to dig for. Now I suggest you go home and sleep off the vast quantities of alcohol you have drunk.'

Kathy got up and walked over to Will.

'Can we go now?'

'Yeah, sure.'

Stanson watched them leave. Why did she not want him but loved a man like that? He had heard the stories about Sergeant Will Falco, all the women and the arrogant attitude, but professionally he couldn't help but admire him and hope one day he could be that good, and he hated the mental conflict this created. He knew Kathy was special and now he could only sit and watch someone else be with her. He knew it would only ever be one night.

Chapter 13

Will had taken his car to the ball. It was his pride and joy, a Mustang Shelby GT 500. It was all black with silver. He didn't get to drive it often, but he had tonight as he didn't want to ride his motorcycle in his designer suit.

'This is yours?'

'Yeah, of course.'

'Never seen it before, that's all.'

'It would get a bit too much attention at the PD if I drove it to work, don't you think? and it would invite so many questions.'

'Yeah, that's true. The guys would be all over it and wanting to take it for a spin.' She paused as she got in the passenger side. 'Can I ask you a personal question?'

'Of course, anything.'

'Well, someone said the ball has been going for five years.'

'Well, as it is now yeah, but it has been going for years before that.'

'So, do you pay for all that?'

'You mean the ball, right?'

'Yeah, of course, what else?'

'Then in all honesty, yes. I wanted to give something back to the PD and it was something I could do after my parents died.'

'That's sweet.'

'Don't spread that around. I have a reputation to protect, don't want anyone thinking I'm a soft touch,'

Kathy laughed, and he smiled. It had been an amazing night.

Kathy was enjoying the ride home, music playing, and she was so relaxed.

'So, what did Richards want?' Will asked after a while.

'Nothing much, she was drunk, and has a serious crush on you, by the way, and she said I wasn't good enough for you.'

'Really, you're not the first person to tell me that about her, and I think you are more than good enough for me.'

'I'm glad about that.'

They pulled up outside Kathy's house, and Will put the roof up on the car and they walked up the steps, hand in hand. When they got inside Will went to the window and closed the blinds and took off his suit jacket and tie. Kathy poured two glasses of wine and put them on the coffee table. Will sat.

'I shouldn't really drink that, I'm on call tomorrow.'

'You can have a bit.'

'So, did you enjoy yourself tonight?'

'Yeah, I did, especially when I got to leave with you.'

'That was my favourite part too.'

She looked at him, and he moved closer to her and was about to kiss her when she spoke.

'Look, Will, I think we need to talk first because I don't want things to be a problem again.'

'OK, but it could wait till morning.'

'If I don't say what I need to now I may not say it at all.'

Will sat back on the sofa, and she sat at the edge and had a drink of wine before she continued.

'That night in the bar with Richards, I sort of knew about the women before me but I never really dealt with it because of the shooting. When you kissed me before I was taken, it was like a dream come true for me. I never thought I could live up to any of them and then when Richards started going on about it, I started to question it myself.'

'OK, I understand that, but there were good reasons why I never stayed with those women.'

'I know, but then the fact you weren't talking to me either, it all got too much and I couldn't deal with that, and the stress with the new team.'

'Kathy, I understand, I was meaning to tell you everything for weeks and there just never seemed to be the right time. I care so much about you and I didn't handle things very well, I know that.'

Kathy finished her glass of wine and got up to pour another.

'You know you need to thank Gina, right,' she said from the kitchen.

'What for?'

'She has been on my back for weeks about why I hadn't sorted things out with you, and she had a right go at me over all that with the captain, which I am very sorry for by the way.'

'It doesn't matter. I know how I can be sometimes, and I have a different way of dealing with stuff. Stanson just got the bad side of it, that's all.'

'You are being awfully nice about all this.'

'It doesn't matter any more, not now.'

Kathy took her shoes off. She almost tripped over her dress as she tried to walk back to sit next to Will. He stood up and walked to her; he was right in front of her.

'Let me help you with that,' he said flirtatiously.

He put his arms around her and unzipped her dress. It dropped to the floor. She stepped out of it and unbuttoned his shirt slowly. He took it off and then kissed her. Her heart was racing; she was so nervous. In their months together, they had never made love because of her leg and the recovery. Now she was worried she would not be as good as all the others, but she wanted him more than how much it scared her.

They sat on the sofa. He kissed her again, softly at first then with more passion and urgency. She lay back and he followed her, kissing her neck. He lifted his head and looked at her.

'Are we OK doing this here?'

'Yeah, tried and tested.'

Will sat up quickly and looked at her, puzzled. She suddenly realised what she had said. Will stood up and stepped away from the sofa, but turned back to look at her. She sat up, suddenly very aware she was in her underwear.

'I meant because it's new; you only got this last month.'

He walked towards the kitchen. Kathy got up and followed him. He faced the wall his hands on the side. She touched his back. He turned around.

'I am thinking I know the answer, but who?'

'Does it matter?'

'To me, yeah, when we were together, I waited for you to be ready and then you have a one-night stand in between us being together. I think I have a right to know.'

'It was a mistake. Thursday night I was in a lot of pain after all the training this week, so I took some of my painkillers the hospital gave me, then after you had been, I was a little upset so I had a drink. I was a bit drunk so he helped me tidy up and then one thing led to another. It was a mistake; I would never have done it sober.'

'It was Stanson though, right?'

'Yeah it was.' She looked down.

Will sighed, then he lifted her face to look at him. He smiled.

'It's OK, we weren't together. Am I disappointed? Yes. Could I rip his head off? Probably, but we are moving forward, together, right? And I can hardly comment about having a one-night stand, can I? Now, tell me, did he go to bed with you?'

'No.'

'Then let's go.'

She smiled and followed him up the stairs.

***

Kathy woke the next morning and stretched. The other side of the bed was empty. She looked around but Will wasn't there. She grabbed something to put on and went downstairs. Will was in the kitchen; he had tidied up the clothes and glasses from last night and had made coffee. She put her arms around him. He was wearing just a pair of jeans.

'Good morning,' he said, leaning down and kissing her on the forehead.

'Good morning, you know you didn't have to tidy up. You could have stayed in bed.'

'As good as that sounds, I was on call from eight, so I have to be ready to go in at any time, you know that.' He walked across to the sofa and put his T-shirt on.

'Where did you get the clothes?'

'My car.'

'You have spare clothes in your car?'

'Yeah.'

'You were that sure you wouldn't be going home?'

'No, I always have spare clothes, in case I crash at Tom's or something.'

'So, what did you want to do today?' Kathy asked, having a drink of coffee.

'Well, I have something planned, if that's OK.'

'And what's that?'

'A surprise, so when you're showered and dressed, we can go.'

Half an hour later she was ready to go. She was wearing skinny jeans and a top, but Will looked at her like she was the most beautiful woman on earth. She locked the door and followed Will to the car.

'So, do I not get a clue?'

'You said you wanted to know me, right?' He unlocked the car. 'So get in and you will.'

They drove for about twenty minutes and they turned into a cemetery. Kathy looked at Will but he stayed focussed. He pulled over after a few minutes and got out. Kathy got out. He walked round the car and took her hand. They walked down a path and stopped by a tree.

'I wanted you to meet my parents,' Will said.

Kathy looked at the headstones side by side and read the inscriptions. There were beautiful fresh flowers in vases on each. She turned to Will.

'I don't know what to say.'

'You don't have to say anything. I wanted you to see them and understand it, I guess. Their death and their lives made me who I am today.'

'They must have been pretty special.'

'Yeah, the best. A lot of people think rich people are arrogant and stuck up, but they weren't, not at all, and so I try to live the same way.'

'Well, I think they would be very proud.'

Will turned to her.

'OK, are you ready to go to one last place?'

'Yeah, of course.'

They went back to the car and headed back to Manhattan, to Will's home. He pulled into the underground garage and pulled in the space next to his motorcycle. He put the roof up, got out and waited for Kathy. They walked up some steps around the corner and through some glass doors.

'Hey, Jimmy, how's it going?'

'Hey, Will, I'm good, how are you?'

'Good, this is Kathy, you may be seeing her around a lot.'

'Hi, Kathy, nice to meet you.'

'You too.'

'See you later, Jimmy.'

Will and Kathy walked to the first elevator. Will pressed the button and the doors opened. He put in a four-digit code and the elevator started moving.

'You have your own elevator?'

'Yeah, only goes to the top. I know it's a bit much but my parents had this put in and the others don't go to my floor.'

'Actually, I like it.'

The elevator reached the top and the door opened. There was a door down from the elevator on the opposite side of the hallway. Will opened it and let Kathy go in first.

'Wow,' she said and stopped. 'I can't believe you live here, and all those nights you were happy to stay at my place.'

'Yeah, I know it's a bit on the large side.'

'It's amazing.'

Will let her wonder around, the living room and kitchen was open plan. There were two doors off it, one was Will's bedroom, which was bigger than the whole of Kathy's downstairs; it had a bathroom and walk-in closet. The other door was a gym. Then off the corridor were three large bedrooms, all with en-suites and a cinema room with ten seats. At the end of the corridor was Will's favourite part, a roof terrace. It was a third of the whole floor with seats, a bar and a barbeque.

'Wow, look at these views, they are amazing.'

'You should see it at night.'

'I bet it's amazing.'

Kathy was so amazed by the whole place. She had never been impressed by money ever in her life but this was so different, this was beyond wealthy.

'So, can we try out the bed?' she said playfully.

'You can stay tonight if you like.'

Just then Will's beeper went.

'Looks like you have to go.'

'Yeah, but if you go home, grab some stuff for tonight and work tomorrow, I will see you back here as soon as I can.' He kissed her and headed inside. She followed.

'Can I watch a movie?'

'Yeah, of course,' he said while collecting his stuff together.

'Can I watch one with Gina?'

Will stopped and looked at her.

'Sorry, I shouldn't have asked that. It's your place. It's OK, I will keep myself busy.'

'No, it's OK, she can come. She knows enough about me and I trust her. I will call you when I am on the way back, OK?' He handed her a piece of paper. 'This is the code for the elevator, don't show it to anyone.'

'OK, see you soon.' She kissed him and he left.

Kathy went and flopped on the sofa, pulled out her phone and dialled.

'Hey, Gina, you will never guess where I am.'

Chapter 14

Will got to the office and the team started to arrive just after him; they were on standby. Tom came straight over.

'So how did it go last night?'

'Good and bad, but this morning was better. I took her to see my parents and she is at mine right now.'

'Wow, really? That's great, but what's the bad?'

'She had sex with Stanson the other night.'

'What seriously?'

'Yeah, she was drinking on painkillers, and he took advantage.'

'She said that?'

'No, she said she was drunk so that's all I need to know.'

'It wasn't rape or anything, though right?'

'Hell, no, he wouldn't be breathing if it was.'

'Fair enough, but take it easy with him because you need to stay good with Kathy and the captain.'

'I know, I will try to resist kicking the shit out of him.'

At that moment Richards walked in. She looked really rough: her hair was a mess, roughly tied back; she had traces of makeup still on her face; she looked like she had barely slept too. Will looked at her then nudged Tom. Tom tried not to laugh when he looked over at her. The rest of the team were not looking, to avoid laughing too; being hung over was a big no on Alpha team. Will walked over and poured a coffee before going over to her desk.

'Richards, you don't look good.'

'I'm fine, Sergeant, ready for duty.'

'I don't think you are. Tom get the breathalyser for me.'

Tom went into Will's office and got it from a drawer. He came back and handed it to Will.

'If you aren't still drunk blow into this.'

'I'm not drunk.'

'Then blow.'

Richards had no choice; she blew into it and Will watched the screen.

'Three times over the limit.'

'No way.'

'Yes, and so you need to go home and hand over your keys because you aren't driving.'

'I drove here.'

'You get behind the wheel and I will have you arrested.' He held out his hand and she gave him her keys. 'Now go, I will have you taken off today's call rota.'

'What! No, I can't afford to lose that money.'

'Then you shouldn't have drunk so much last night, should you? Now get out before I write you up for being unfit for duty.'

'Come on, Sergeant, you can't tell me you haven't done it. I didn't think we would get a call, and it's not like I do anything when we do.'

'No, I haven't done it, because drunk or hung over means I can't do my job properly. I am responsible for saving lives and protecting the public every time I put my uniform on, and I can't and won't turn up for work unless I can do that, which means, like the rest of the team, I only drank soda and alcohol-free drinks last night. Now, if you want to stay on SWAT, or even the force, I suggest you learn fast what we expect from that uniform, and on Alpha team anything less than perfect is not good enough. Now go home and make sure you are sober for tomorrow's shift.'

Richards looked at him. She stood and left without saying another word. Just then the team's beepers went off.

***

They pulled up just off Times Square. There was a number of officers at the scene and the square had been cordoned off, which was causing chaos even on a Sunday.

'My apologies, Sergeant, we have an armed man in the middle of the road, waving a gun around, but he hasn't fired one yet.'

'So why are we here? Sounds easy enough.'

'Because he said he would only surrender to SWAT, so he's all yours.'

Will went over to the team.

'Well, this is a weird one. We have one armed man who says he will give himself up to us.'

'So, what's the catch?'

'No clue, so let's be careful. Tom you go with Bennett and Palmer down onto the next road, Harvey with me. We will go head on to him, take it steady.'

They approached the edge of the block carefully. Will could see the man. He watched him; he was just standing there. Then his phone beeped. He looked at it, then put his gun down on the ground. Will approached him carefully. He handcuffed the man and Harvey walked him away. Will was standing looking around when Tom came over.

'I don't get it,' Tom said.

'Hey, in a world full of crazies, we can't understand them all.'

'Yeah, that's true.'

They walked back to the cars and went back to the office. Will called Kathy on route to say he would be a bit longer and to make sure all was OK. He finished the call, and Tom looked at him.

'Look at you all, in love and stuff.'

'I know it's a surprise to me too.'

'I'm happy for you, it's about time.'

'Yeah, I guess it is.'

***

Richards was at home when her cell phone went. She looked at the screen; it was her brother.

'Hey how did it go?'

'He did exactly what you said, so now what?'

'We plan out the next step. We need to make it as perfect as possible. We can't afford to make any mistakes on this.'

'Do you have someone to do the job?'

'Yes, I do, and he is very good at it too,'

'Won't he be worried going up against this guy?'

'Cops don't scare him, not even Sergeant Falco.'

'So, what do you want me to do?'

'Keep following him and keep doing what you have with Kathy Hill too.'

'OK, sis, I just hope this works.'

'Of course, it will. How could it go wrong? See you later.'

She hung up and smiled.

***

Will got home and he looked around for Kathy and Gina, He checked the cinema room first and then he found them out on the roof terrace looking at the view of Central Park. He crept up behind Kathy, put his arms round her and bent down and kissed her neck softly. She turned around and kissed him.

'OK, that's my signal to leave,' Gina said, finishing her drink.

'No, Gina, you don't have to go,' Kathy replied.

'Yeah, I do. You two need some time alone, but, Will, don't think this means you can avoid our chat.'

'Our chat?'

'Yeah, as to why I have never been here before,' she joked, 'it's truly amazing.'

'Thanks, I will take you down to the lobby.'

'No, it's OK, you don't have to, I can find my own way.'

'Actually, you can't because it's a private elevator and only five people have a code for it.'

'Oh, that's not much good.'

'Well, it's for privacy and security.'

'Yeah, and a pain in the ass if you have to take every visitor down.'

'I don't get that many visitors, but I will call Jimmy and get him to take you down, OK.'

'Yeah, OK, that sounds fine.'

They went back inside and Will called downstairs. There was a buzzing noise for a moment then, after a few minutes, there was a knock at the door. Will opened it and Jimmy was there.

'OK, you two have fun and I will see you both in the office tomorrow.' She left and Will turned to Kathy.

'Why don't you look through the menus in the kitchen. I'm going for a shower, choose whatever you want.'

'OK,' she grabbed him and kissed him, 'but is there any rush?'

'It's getting late and I need a shower. That can wait till later.'

'OK, go before I join you.'

After Will got out of the shower, he put on a pair of shorts and sat next to Kathy on the sofa. She turned and looked at him.

'I have been thinking.'

'Really, do I dare ask?'

'I think we should have your team round for a barbeque.'

'What, here?'

'Yes, here.' She moved to see him better. 'You trust them, don't you? I don't know why you can't let them into the outer circle of your life: the "my parents left me this place", part.'

'You're serious?'

'Of course, I am.'

'And you don't think that more questions will follow them coming here, and I don't trust them all.'

'So, don't invite Richards, but I think the guys that have your back every day deserve some trust and honesty.'

Will looked at her for a moment.

'I guess you're right, they do.'

'Really?' she asked, smiling.

'Yeah, but I decide what they get to know, OK?'

'Yes of course.'

'Good, now you can do something for me in return.'

'I can?'

'Yes, you can.'

'And what's that?' she asked playfully.

'Invite your parents to New York.'

Kathy got up and walked into the kitchen. She turned around to face him and leaned on the kitchen counter. Will followed her and stood opposite.

'Seriously, you know what my mom is like, about my job and my love life. I daren't even tell her what happened because I know how she will react.'

'Yes, I do, and I also know it's time to make it right.'

'Wow, I can't believe you are asking me to do this.'

'What you just asked of me is no walk in the park, Kathy. I have kept my personal life so separate for years now and to let people in and to trust them with this part of me is extremely difficult.' He stepped towards her and took her hands. 'I would do anything to have one last conversation with my parents.'

'Really, playing the guilt card.'

'Let me finish, I know things have been tough but now you have me to be there with you, and you have to do this, or you will regret it if you don't take the opportunity to make things right with them.'

'You know this might not make things right with them, and no, I don't have to but I do need to.'

'OK then, now what did you want for dinner because I am starving?'

Chapter 15

The next day Will was in his office when the team arrived. He went to his door and shouted.

'Hargreaves, Harvey, Bennett, Palmer, my office.'

'Not me, Sergeant?' Richards asked.

'No, because you aren't an active shooter at present, Richards.' He shut the door behind them. It was a tight squeeze to have them all in there.

'OK, the conversation we are about to have goes no further than this room and if it does then I will be looking for new team members.' He suddenly smiled. 'Kathy and I want you all to come for a barbeque on Saturday at my place.'

'Your place?' Harvey asked.

'Yes, and bring Selena and Lynne.'

'But we don't know where you live.'

'I know that, Bennett, you will find out on Saturday. Now get to work and don't say a word to Richards.'

As the others left, Tom stopped in the doorway.

'Are you sure about this?'

'Yeah, it's about time I started being more honest with people I trust and have my back every day.'

'OK then.'

As Tom walked back across the office, the captain appeared.

'Falco, just the man, I want you to go and help Sergeant Hill today on the range. They have a week to qualify and they are not quite there yet, so go and help. Also, I have to pass on a thank you from the chief; whatever you said to those parents in court last week, they have dropped the case and are no longer pursuing criminal charges, so good work.'

'That's good news, Captain, but all I did was tell them the truth.'

'Well, it obviously worked.' He went back to his office.

***

Kathy was on the range already helping Blain. Will walked down to the other end. Stanson and Ford were talking.

'How are you after Saturday night?' Ford asked Stanson.

'Fine, why?'

'After the display between Sergeant Hill and Sergeant Falco. We all know you have a bit of a crush on her.'

'Well, I think that she can do better than that arrogant prick, and yes, I think she is amazing and I can make her happy, but she chose him for now at least,' Stanson answered.

Will stood behind them and coughed. Ford and Stanson turned around, saw him and turned back. Stanson fired down the range at his target. Will moved behind him and said quietly, 'I know what you did. How does it feel to know she will only have sex with you when she is drunk and you take advantage?'

Will started to move away.

'You think you are so fucking perfect, don't you? Believe you are better than me. Well I'm not scared of you!' Stanson shouted.

Will turned around to see Stanson pointing his gun at him.

'Here's two things I know: you should never point a gun at me that has an empty clip, and you should first make sure I'm not armed.'

Will pulled his gun and pointed it at Stanson. Kathy noticed what was happening and walked over.

'What the hell is going on?'

Stanson looked at her and lowered his gun. Will turned and fired down the range. He retrieved his target and Stanson's and put them in front of Stanson.

'Now we know who is better, and touch my girlfriend again and that is what will happen to you.'

'Sergeant Falco, a word outside please,' Kathy demanded.

Will followed Kathy off the range.

'What the fuck was that, Will?'

'He pulled his at me first.'

'And you knew it was empty.' She paused. 'And don't think I didn't hear what you just said either.'

'I was just…'

'Marking your territory.'

'No.'

'Then what?'

'I was just letting him know you are off limits now.'

'Really?'

'OK, and that I knew he took advantage.'

'What the fuck, I knew you weren't OK about this.'

'I'm OK with you having sex when you are single. Well, I can't deny I would have preferred it be someone else, but I'm not OK with what he did.'

'Will, it was my choice. Even if I was drunk you have no right. Just because I was kidnapped and shot, it doesn't mean I need saving all the time or that I can't handle myself.'

'I know you can handle yourself; I find it really sexy actually.'

'Don't try and sweet talk me when I'm mad at you.'

He stepped forward and kissed her on the head.

'I just wanted to watch your back.'

'I know, but this is my team, Will, and I need to handle things my way. Now do you think you can play nice while I talk to Stanson?'

'Yeah, I can do that, unless you had sex with anyone else in there.'

'That's not funny.'

Will walked back onto the range and Kathy asked Stanson to step out.

'So, I have heard one side, what's yours?'

'I'm sure Sergeant Falco covered everything.'

'No, he told me his story and now I want yours.'

'He knows what happened between us.'

'Yes, he does.'

'Well, he used that to belittle me and I snapped.'

'OK, well first of all pointing a gun at a sergeant, especially Falco, is not a good idea.'

'Yeah, I have got that.'

'Good, because next time you might not be so lucky.'

'I just don't understand what you see in him.'

'Stanson, it's not for you to understand. My personal life is exactly that and we were a big mistake. Now, if you can't work professionally on my team and alongside Sergeant Falco's, maybe SWAT isn't the best fit for you.'

'Yes, Sergeant.'

'Now, Sergeant Falco is literally the best on this unit. You can learn a lot from him and his team, but that choice is yours. Do you want this job?'

'Yes, Sergeant.'

'Then get back on that range, we have a week.'

Will's beeper went off so he left Kathy and her team and went up to the office. Tom was walking out as he got there.

'Shots fired at a shopping mall.'

'OK, let's go.'

They took the truck to a small mall just outside the city centre. It had been evacuated so there was a lot of people standing around watching what was happening. Will got out and headed straight to the sergeant in charge, as he always did.

'Sergeant Falco, good to see you,' said Sergeant Green. 'We have three female suspects in a clothing store on the first floor. They aren't answering the phone so we don't know what they want.'

'All females, that's a new one.'

'Yeah, I know but that's what we got.'

Will headed back to the team, thinking about how to tackle it, He made a call to the captain, and minutes later Kathy arrived, all suited up.

'OK, now we are ready.'

The team looked at him and then at Kathy, then back at Will.

'We have three female suspects so I needed a female officer to go in with us.'

'What am I?' exclaimed Richards.

'You are an officer with a bad aim, and I don't trust you to have my back.'

'That's hardly fair you never give me a chance.'

'You had one. You haven't improved at all on the range. You are just as likely to hit one of us, so Sergeant Hill is coming in on this one.'

Richards walked off and took out her phone and made a call.

'So, Palmer and Harvey, you will cover the entrance, Bennett and Tom, you go in and move to the left, me and Sergeant Hill will go straight in and cover the right.'

They made their way to the store. The mall was empty and the suspects hadn't opened fire at anyone on their way in so there were no injuries or fatalities, but there was damage to the building where they had fired. When they got to the entrance, the team stayed low so they didn't get spotted till they were in a good position. The three suspects were near the counter and they were definitely armed. One was pointing a handgun at the person behind the counter. They got as close as they could before Will announced their presence.

'NYPD, put your weapons down and put your hands on your head.'

The three women turned to face the team, now pointing their weapons right at them.

'Oh, look a bunch of police with guns. You shoot us and we will let the world know you are just men trying to oppress us women.'

'I figured you may try and play something like that; it's why I brought her,' Will replied, gesturing towards Kathy.

'Now what?' one of the women said to the other.

'Now you put your weapons down,' Will insisted.

'I don't think we will.'

'OK, last chance, lower your weapons or we will fire.'

'You won't fire because we are women and that will make you look bad,' said the main suspect. 'Bringing a female won't change that.'

'So, what's new.' He signalled to Kathy. She fired, hitting the other suspect in the shoulder, and she fell to the floor. The main suspect turned to aim at Kathy.

'You shouldn't have done that.'

The suspect was about to fire, but Will did first, and she fell to the floor. The other suspect tried to run but ran straight into Tom who arrested her.

'Control, this is Alpha team, we are all clear. We need EMTs for an injured suspect.'

'Received, Alpha team.'

Kathy went over to Will and they looked at the suspect.

'You didn't have to shoot her in the head, you know.'

'I told you, I will always have your back.' He looked at Kathy. 'She would have fired.'

'I know,' she smiled at him, 'and thanks for the call I have missed being out in the field.'

'Only a week and you will be out here too, leading your own team. Now that will be pretty special.'

'Yeah, I know, and at least I will work alongside you.'

***

When they got back to the office, Captain Bridge was waiting for them.

'I need you two in my office.'

They followed and went in to see Stanson sitting there. Will stood by the door and Kathy sat down.

'Now, Stanson here has been filling me in to an extent about a few issues and an incident that happened on the range earlier.'

'Really?'

'Yes, Falco, he has. Now, Stanson, go back to your training while I talk to my sergeants.'

Stanson got up and left, not making eye contact with either Kathy or Will as he left.

'Falco, take a seat.'

'I would rather stand, Captain.'

'Well I would rather you sit.'

Will sat next to Kathy; he knew this was not going to be good.

'Now, I want you both to listen and let me finish before you say anything.' They both nodded so he continued. 'OK, well, Stanson has made a verbal report to me that Falco here is going out of his way to be intimidating and aggressive towards him. Now, we spoke not that long ago that you had to start playing nice or I would have to do something. I'm sorry, Falco, but I am going to have to put you at your desk for the rest of today and tomorrow.'

'What?' Kathy said.

'Now hang on, Captain, my team are already down one. I can't be out of the field right now.'

'Yes, Sergeant, you can. Sergeant Hill will head your team and you will train hers.'

Will really needed to punch something but he had known this was coming if he stepped out of line. Kathy sat for a moment before she spoke.

'Captain, can I speak with you alone?'

'Of course. Falco, you can leave.'

Will left, a bit confused. He saw Stanson and left the office quickly and headed for the gym before he used Stanson as a punch bag.

'Did Stanson tell you everything, Captain?'

'I'm not sure what you mean, Sergeant.'

'OK, we had sex on Thursday night.'

'You and Stanson?'

'Yeah, and I know I'm not supposed to be involved with my team but it was just once. Anyway, on Saturday me and Will sorted things out. He found out what had happened and because I was drunk, he thinks Stanson took advantage. So Stanson made a comment about him being better for me than Will, so Will said something. Stanson pointed his weapon at Will and then Will pulled his. I spoke to them both and thought this was sorted till you called us in. You can't take Will out of the field; you need him out there. He thinks fast and is the best at watching anyone's back.'

'Well, I have to say this changes a few things; you are risking a lot telling me this.'

'It won't happen again. Will would actually kill him, and I have no desire to be with anyone else but Will.'

'OK, but this needs resolving.'

'I have an idea but you need to give them no choice on this and it didn't come from me.'

'OK, tell me more.'

Chapter 16

Kathy went to find Will, though she knew where he would be, where he always was when he was stressed or pissed off. He was in the gym, punching the bag. It was a very functional space with plenty of space and equipment to keep the teams in top condition. It was Will's haven when anything got too much for him. She watched him for a moment, in his work trousers but shirtless. His physique was enough to make many women go weak, never mind his good looks that went with that. She felt her heart flutter as she walked over.

'Captain, wants you.'

'Why, what did I do now?'

'Nothing, I don't think.'

Will stopped and looked at her. She was smiling.

'What are you smiling at?'

'Nothing, but you may want to put a shirt on before you go upstairs.'

'My clean shirts are upstairs,' he replied, wiping himself down with a towel.

'Yeah, and so is Richards.'

'Are you saying you don't want other women looking at me?'

'No, I'm saying I don't trust her,' she sighed, 'and you know the other week when you walked across the office like that?'

'Yeah.'

'The officer I was interviewing asked if all SWAT look like you and how closely she would be working with you. Apparently, you are a legend at her precinct.'

'Really? You should have signed her up.' He smiled.

'I don't think so.'

'Are you jealous, Sergeant? Or do you want me all to yourself?'

'I'm not jealous. Now come on, the captain's waiting.'

They headed up to the locker room, avoiding the office as they did so; no one was in there. Will opened his locker. Kathy stood next to it, leaning on the one next to it.

'So where are your recruits?'

'Writing reports.'

'So, you don't have to watch them or should I say I don't.'

'No, they can do them just fine, they are police officers already.' She looked at him as he was looking in his bag for a clean shirt.

'What?'

'Nothing,' she said, 'just thinking about later.'

'Really?' He moved closer to her and leaned forward and started gently kissing her neck, then up to her mouth. She responded and she could feel herself wanting him right there. She stopped suddenly.

'I don't think this is a good idea.'

'Are you sure because your increased heart rate and breathing would say differently.'

'I didn't say I didn't want you, I said it wasn't a good idea, even when you are stood here half dressed.'

He moved away, picked up his clean shirt and put it on.

'Better?'

'Better, now go and see the captain.'

'You do know what he wants.'

'No,' she laughed.

'OK, if you say so,' he said as he left, and went into the office. Kathy took a deep breath and composed herself before she followed.

'Captain, you wanted to see me,' Will said as he went in the captain's office, then he saw Stanson sitting there.

'Yes, Falco, come in.'

Will shut the door and stood arms folded.

'Sit down, Sergeant.'

'I'm OK standing, Captain.'

'It's not a request, Sergeant; you make me feel uneasy when you are towering over me like that.'

Will sat down next to Stanson and folded his arms once more.

'Now firstly, I have had a chat with Sergeant Hill and got a few things straight. Stanson, when you make a serious complaint against one of my sergeants make sure I get all the facts because I don't enjoy looking stupid. Sergeant Falco, after the new information I have received, you are back on duty. However, due to that same information I need to change things around. Fremont who was going to join Alpha will now be Sergeant Hill's number two and Stanson here will be joining Alpha.'

'Are you kidding?'

'No, Sergeant, I'm not. Stanson can no longer be part of Hill's team after their intimate and sexual relations, so I don't have a choice.'

'Don't I get a say as to who joins Alpha?'

'Well, Sergeant, you would have, had this not happened, but now you can either have Stanson or keep Richards.'

'That's the only choice?'

'The other will go to Price's team as they are one down with Dune going, so you get to choose which you would prefer.'

'Neither are Alpha standard, Captain.'

'So, pick the one you can train to be Alpha standard then.'

'Well, that's not Richards, she has proved that over the last few weeks.'

'Then, Stanson, you are now Alpha team, at least you are when you qualify. Sergeant Falco, you will oversee his training when you aren't out on a call. He has a week to be ready.'

'Captain, don't I have choice?' Stanson asked.

'Yes, join Alpha or don't join SWAT.'

'But I'm fine where I am. I can be completely professional.'

'What like today on the range?' He stood up. 'Now get back to work both of you and I don't expect any more issues between you two.'

Will and Stanson left the captain's office. They stopped by Will's office door.

'Get ready, Stanson, because from tomorrow I own your ass, and as you may have heard, I expect the best.'

'Yes, Sergeant, I will try my best.' He left the office and went back to the training room.

Will saw Kathy in her office. He went in and closed the door.

'Why do I think you had something to do with that?'

'With what?' she said, looking up from her paperwork.

'You know what, the staff change,' he said as he sat on her desk.

'Ah that, then maybe.'

'I don't get why you told him, about you and Stanson.'

'Because you shouldn't have been on desk duty, and I actually think you two will work together quite well, once you trust him.'

'So, you could have got in trouble for me.'

'Yes, basically.'

'Why?'

'Because, Will Falco,' she stood and walked round the desk to him, 'I love you.'

'I love you too,' he said, then he kissed her. He held her tightly and she responded to his touch. He stopped and looked at her.

'Sorry, I know I shouldn't do that here.'

'Really, Will, because the increased heart rate and breathing say differently.' She smiled.

He smiled back at her, then went to kiss her again and his beeper went off.

'Great timing as always.' He got up and walked over and opened the door. 'Are you going to wait here if it runs over shift?'

'Yeah, I have some paperwork to do.'

Will stepped out and his team were ready to go.

'Richards, you stay here, shift's almost over so you can go home.'

They left the office and got in the cars and drove off.

'So, we have officers needing assistance and shots fired at a warehouse in Queens.'

'OK, on it.' Tom put the sirens on and floored it.

***

Richards went into Kathy's office.

'Listen, I'm sorry about Saturday night, Sergeant, I was a little drunk.'

'That's OK, say no more about it,' Kathy said without looking up from her paperwork.

Richards stood for a moment, trying to work out what to say to engage Kathy in a conversation.

'It's tough being a woman here, isn't it?'

'Really, I've never found that. I have always just felt like part of the family, especially within Alpha team.'

'Oh, what's your secret?'

'Work hard, learn and don't expect to be treated any different to the men.' She put her pen down and looked up. 'The team have to know they can trust you, that you have their back. You shouldn't give up hope on yourself or the team. You are new to SWAT and to get an Alpha team spot is tough but, Richards, if you don't work hard and improve, they will kick you off SWAT. You don't want that, do you?'

'No, of course not. I don't suppose you want a drink later to talk about how I can get better, do you?'

'I'm sorry I can't, I have plans tonight, but I would be happy to, another night though, OK?'

'Yeah sure.'

***

As Will got to the scene with the team, there were bullets flying everywhere. They jumped out of their cars and took cover. They always got ready on route for these kinds of calls because they never knew what they were driving into. There were squad cars and unmarked cars with officers hiding behind them. Will couldn't ask what was going on; he needed to act and fast.

'Holy shit, I really hate these!' Tom shouted.

'OK, I need cover fire from White, Yellow and Blue. Red and Green move forward. Let's flush these guys out,' Will radioed. With all the gunshots they couldn't hear him otherwise.

Palmer, Bennett and Harvey provided cover fire. Will and Tom moved forward low. They took out the first two men at the doorway of the building.

'Alpha team, move forward.'

As they did so they came under fire again from another two men who appeared. Harvey took one and then Palmer another. They got to the door and went inside, before they were fired upon again. They worked their way through the whole building, which took some time. Every time they took out two suspects, another two seemed to appear, and they were good, nearly hit the team a few times, but they worked their way through, taking out twelve suspects in all. Another four gave up as they ran out of ammo. Unlike the team they fired a lot of bullets while Will's team only needed one for each suspect and fired very few others. It was a drug manufacturing and dealing den. There were hundreds of packets of white powder piled up ready to go; this was a large seizure.

'Control, this is Alpha team, we are all clear.'

'Received, Alpha team.'

Tom walked over and picked up one of the packets.

'This is ready to go out: got here at a good time.'

Just then a detective walked in and over to the team.

'Thanks, guys, we knew we had to get them tonight before this hit the streets but we weren't expecting this kind of resistance.'

'Glad we could help,' Will replied. 'Let's go, guys, our work here is done.'

***

They got back to the office; it was very quiet. The two teams on shift were out on other calls, and all Kathy's team and Richards had already gone home.

'OK, guys, go home, you can write up in the morning.'

'Don't have to tell us twice. See you tomorrow, Sergeant.'

They all left, chatting about going for a drink after they were changed. It had been more regular for them to do so recently as the shifts seemed to be getting more stressful. Will poured a coffee and went and stood in Kathy's doorway. He watched her while drinking his coffee.

'So, are you ready to go?'

'Yeah, just about.'

Will went into her office, put his cup on the desk and walked round till he was behind her. He leaned forward and put his arms around her and kissed the back of her neck softly and slowly.

'Can you not wait for five minutes? I am nearly finished and this is for you. It's Stanson's file, all up to date for you.'

'Well, that's a name that will ruin a moment.'

He walked back round to the other side of her desk, picked up his cup and finished his coffee. Kathy closed the file and got up and she walked round to him. She took his hands and looked at him.

'Let's get changed, go home, eat and go to bed.' She smiled. 'We can talk about work tomorrow.'

Will smiled at her.

'Now, that's the best offer I've had all day.'

Chapter 17

The next day Will and Kathy had the recruits in the gym, working them all hard. Will had a number of fitness workouts that he had put together over the years and Kathy was taking advantage and using them as part of her training. Stanson was doing extremely well, and Will was quietly impressed with his fitness, though he was not ready to say that out loud till he trusted him a little more.

'So, what do you think?' Kathy asked as they leaned against the wall at the other end of the gym watching them all.

'He's OK, at least he will keep up, not like Richards.'

'Really, just OK, can't admit you might have been wrong?'

'I would rather wait on that because I haven't been proven wrong yet.'

'Wow, really?'

'Yes, really, I mean, look at the way he is hitting that bag, for a start.'

'Male ego is something I will never understand.'

'Nothing to do with it.'

'If you say so, I mean, look at his body.'

'Look at his body?' Will moved and looked at her.

'Yeah, I mean he keeps pretty fit.'

'Are you serious right now?'

'Not jealous, are you, Sergeant?'

'What, that my girlfriend is eyeing up a guy she had sex with, and telling me how fit he is, no, of course not.'

'Will, I was joking, he has nothing on you. Now why don't you get that shirt off and go and show him how it's done.'

Will laughed and went across the gym to Stanson, taking off his shirt as he did so. If he was joining Alpha, he needed to get much better. Kathy watched them, smiling.

***

They were up in the office about an hour later. Will was organising Stanson by moving Richards over to Price's team desks. He introduced him properly to all the team.

'Tom, can you go and see Wayne and get his weapons put with ours and have orange call sign reassigned to him please, so we are ready to go as soon as he has passed on Monday.'

'I'm orange though,' Richards stated.

'Price doesn't use colours. He will allocate you your own call sign so you won't need it now; as of tomorrow you are on Delta team.'

'I will go and do that now, Sergeant,' Tom said.

Tom left to sort it out and the team were talking. Will could see that Stanson would get on well with the team. He seemed to get on particularly well with Harvey, which was good as he could learn from his experience, but he was hoping Stanson would be better, more like he was when he joined; he had high hopes for him. Bennett and Palmer were not leaders, Harvey and Tom weren't interested in moving up, and one day Will would retire so he needed someone to take over.

After twenty minutes of chatting, their beepers went off. The team got up to head out.

'No, Richards, you stay here. Stanson you want to observe?'

'Yeah, of course.'

'Come on then.'

Kathy came out of her office for a coffee as they left. Her team were going over tactics and writing plans for scenarios in the training room so it was just her and Richards. She was sitting at her new desk, looking miserable.

'You know, Delta team is not so bad, a good place to learn.'

'Yeah, I guess so.'

'Do you want to go for that drink tonight. We can chat about you moving and stuff.'

'Yeah, that would be fab, thanks, Sergeant.'

'Sure, no worries.'

***

The team arrived at the scene, a small building with an armed suspect on the second floor. It was in mid-town, a quiet street, by the look of it possibly a small business, looking at the building and those surrounding it. Will went over to the officer in charge.

'Sergeant Falco, we have a suspect and he is talking to officers, just outside the door, but we aren't getting anywhere. He has two hostages that we know of.'

'OK, so where do you want us?'

'On the roof opposite.'

'So, you want a sniper team.' Will smiled.

'Yes, Sergeant, we do, that's why we called you. We have officers inside but we need a backup to get those hostages out.'

'OK, we are on it.'

Will walked back to the truck and got out his sniper rifle. He didn't get to use it much; he was sent into more buildings these days.

'Harvey, grab your sniper. Stanson, you can come up too. Hargreaves, stay down here with the others and cover the ground.'

Harvey and Stanson followed him up the stairs and Will and Harvey set up.

'Alpha team are in place.'

'Received, Alpha team, you have a green light.'

'Green light? So quickly? I mean, we only just got here,' Stanson stated.

'Yeah, if negotiations aren't working, we weren't the first on scene. They have been trying to talk him down for a while. That's why they called us. We have to protect the lives of the hostages, and if the officers inside aren't getting anywhere, going in could force him to shoot one. Though sometimes we have to go in, like if it's on a high floor or wrong kind of windows.'

'OK, so why are there two of you up here?'

'Because it can take a while for a clear shot so we take it in turns.'

'Sorry for all the questions.'

'No, Stanson, don't apologise, it's how to learn,' Will said.

'Sergeant, I can see the target but I can't get a clear shot without hitting a hostage.'

'OK, we can wait a while longer.'

About twenty minutes passed and the suspect moved.

'Sergeant, he's moved slightly but I'm not sure I can make the shot.'

'OK, let me look.'

Will took over and looked through his scope.

'Just watch this,' Harvey said to Stanson.

A shot rang out.

'Control, the suspect is down; it is all clear for the officers to go in.'

'Received, Alpha team.'

Will got up and they started to pack away.

'You see, Stanson, Sergeant Falco made that shot but I knew I couldn't.'

'Why not though?'

'The hostage was really close to him and my margin of error is a lot bigger than his.'

'A lot bigger?'

'Yeah, you can see it better on a target because you can see the holes from the rounds, but I am up to six millimetres out and Sergeant Falco has a near-perfect shot at around two millimetres.'

'That's not a lot though.'

'It is when you have a hostage in sight too. You just can't afford to miss. We have one of the best records for not injuring hostages.'

'Don't worry, Stanson, we will be going up to the sniper range this week; you can have a go then. We all have to be trained on sniper, because for calls like today we are the ones that turn out because Alpha is the designated sniper team, though some teams have one. Bravo have Sergeant Hill; she was trained while she was on Alpha,' Will said as they walked towards the roof door.

They all went back down the stairs and out onto the street. There was an argument erupting between an officer and a woman in front of the building. Will went over, handing his rifle to Tom as he did so.

'What's the issue here?' Will asked the woman.

'The issue is that a man has just been shot in my offices, there is blood everywhere, a body bleeding and I have a bullet hole through my window.'

'OK, well, the coroner is on his way, and you will be able to have it cleaned at the latest of tomorrow.'

'That's not good enough. It's bad enough a mad man caused all this but I thought the police were supposed to sort these things out, not make them worse.'

'Ma'am, we resolved the situation in the best way we could and—'

'Really, if that's the best way I would hate to see the worst.'

'Look, I can try and get a time for the coroner.'

'So, I have to stand around and just wait for them, and what about all the blood?'

'OK, listen, I know a guy who can come in and clean it tonight; here's his card,' Will said, handing it over.

'And how much is that going to cost me? It looks like a slaughter house up there and what about the window?'

Will looked at the woman and tried to stay calm. He knew if he got agitated it would make her worse.

'Call the number, and I will organise someone to come and get the window sorted. I know it's an inconvenience all this, and I'm sorry this happened but we were doing our job to get your staff out safe. Now, why don't you go and get a drink at the coffee shop on the corner and the PD will get this body removed by the coroner and come and get you after that.'

She sighed and looked at Will. She was still angry but nodded in agreement.

'OK, thanks, Officer...'

'Sergeant Falco.'

'Thank you, Sergeant.' She walked off.

Suddenly a woman came running over to Will.

'Will Falco, as I live and breathe, how are you?'

'Hi, Constance, I'm good. How are you?'

'I'm good, I mean, except all this. Did you help?'

'I was on the team that was responsible for getting you out.'

'Well, thank you. So, are you still single?'

'No, actually I'm not.'

'Oh, that's a shame because I was looking for an escort to the summer party schedule; wondered why we haven't seen you out on the scene for a while.'

'I have been a little busy, but maybe I can help you.'

'How so?'

'One of my team is single, fun and very much looking for a woman like you that he can go out and enjoy some time with.'

'Really?'

'Yes, and he can take you out for coffee on Sunday.'

'Which one is he?'

'Bennett, come here.' Bennett walked over to them. 'Bennett, this is Constance and she is going to meet you for coffee on Sunday.'

'OK, hi, nice to meet you.'

'Hi, here's my card, call me, OK?'

'Yeah, of course.'

Constance walked off, smiling.

'Now, Bennett, don't mess this up or you will never date again in this city, because she is very well connected.'

They walked back to the truck, Bennett holding the card like it was made of gold.

***

They got back to the office; Kathy was packing up for the day. Will went in her office.

'How did it go?' she asked, looking up.

'Was a sniper call, so good as always. Stanson asked a lot of questions; he is learning.'

'See, I told you he was a good fit.'

'Yeah, well, a day at a time.'

'Are you going to ask him to come on Saturday?'

'Why would I?'

'He's Alpha now, right?'

'And I've known him for two minutes. Are you ready to go home?'

'No, I'm going for a drink with Richards.'

'Seriously? Why?'

'To see if we have got her wrong or find out her play.'

'You want me to come?'

'No, that will ruin it.'

'OK, call me when you are done and I will pick you up.'

'OK, fine, and have a think about Saturday.'

***

Kathy and Richards walked over to Charlie's bar. It was a bit busy; it appeared to be someone's birthday. They both went to the bar and got a drink, then walked over to the window and sat down.

'Thanks for coming for a drink, Sergeant.'

'It's OK, if it will help you adapt here, I don't mind.'

'Well, I guess I am just finding SWAT a lot harder than I thought I would.'

'But you passed the exams and worked on the unit in Denver. It can't be that different, can it?'

'It's a lot tougher here. in Denver we didn't get the level of calls you do here. I mean, I was not on the Alpha team but it was generally a lot quieter there.'

'You need to focus, Richards; listen to what you are being taught. You won't last long if you don't improve and the captain will be paying attention.'

'OK, I will try, but the exercise side I can't say I will ever get used to that. My body is literally aching all the time.'

'It's part of the job, with all the skyscrapers and multi-level buildings here, our fitness has to stay at its best.'

'Must have been hard for you coming back with your leg and all.'

'Yeah, I can be in a lot of pain some days but it is getting stronger and I am still doing extra exercises to strengthen it too.'

'That's good, and I bet Sergeant Falco is really supportive too.'

'He is, but I got where I am on my own.'

'But he taught you and spent the time to do that.'

'Sometimes, but Tom did his fair share too. Sergeant Falco is the best shot but Tom has so much more patience, especially if you are learning, and maybe if you hadn't disobeyed an order on your first call, Sergeant Falco may have helped you a bit more, because disobeying him is the best way to piss him off. He worked hard to be a sergeant and to take over Alpha team.'

'I noticed that and now it's too late. He is not interested in me at all now.'

'Price is a good officer: you can learn a lot from him. He worked on Alpha for a while, but prefers the less stressful approach of Delta and now it's his team. I think it will be a good fit for you; it won't be quite as busy either.'

'Yeah, maybe it will. I will have to make the most of the opportunity I am given and not regret those that didn't work out.'

'Yeah, that's right.'

They sat and drank their drinks in relative silence, and then Kathy made her excuses and left. She didn't want to hang around waiting for Will so she got a cab.

***

Will was in his gym when Kathy got back; she stood at the doorway. Will stopped and looked at her.

'Thought I was picking you up.'

'I got a cab, it's fine.'

'So how did it go?'

'OK, though she definitely has other reasons for being here and not to be on SWAT but I have no idea what they are.'

'Well, she's Price's problem now.'

'Yes, she is I suppose. So, did you get the food and drinks sorted out for Saturday?'

'There's only eight of us, so it didn't take much sorting really.'

'Eight, you're not inviting Stanson then?'

'No.'

'But…'

'But what?'

'Nothing, I just thought you were getting along.'

'Yeah, so, I am not going to trust him just yet, not that much.'

'I trust him.'

'It's not your decision, Kathy.'

'So, I have no say at all.'

'Honestly, no, it's my life not yours that he is being trusted with.

'Your life? You don't have one, Will. You hide everything from everyone; no one even knows who you are.'

'Wow, I can't believe this. I thought you understood.'

'I do but…'

'But what, you changed your mind?'

'No, Will, I just don't want our lives to be defined by your lack of trust.'

'I'm trying, Kathy. Do you know how hard it is for me to have the team come here? But that's not good enough for you; you just push for more that I'm not ready to give.'

'Yeah well, I'm sorry. I wanted us to have friends.' She paused. 'I think I will stay at mine tonight.' She left.

Will heard the front door close. He punched the bag so hard; he was furious with her and, surprisingly, himself.

When Kathy got outside, she called the only person who really knew Will, and she knew she could talk to.

'Tom, can I pop round? It's really important.'

'Yeah, sure, see you soon.'

Chapter 18

Two hours later, Will was still up, but was about to go to bed when there was a knock at the door. It was Kathy.

'Hi,' Will was surprised to see her, 'thought you was going home.'

'Well, I changed my mind. Is that OK?'

'Of course, I was just going to bed.'

Kathy stepped inside and closed the door behind her.

'Listen, I'm sorry.' She took his hand. 'I shouldn't have pushed you so hard; it was completely unfair of me.'

'I appreciate that but it's OK. I may have over reacted a little bit.'

'No, you didn't, you have been through a lot and I should have been more understanding about that.'

'Hang on, you've been talking to Tom, haven't you?'

Kathy walked away from him; she didn't want to get Tom into any trouble for telling her the whole story. Will followed her and turned her to face him.

'Haven't you?'

'OK, yes, but don't have a go at Tom. I needed to understand and asked the questions. He was only trying to help.'

'It's OK, I have always struggled to talk about what happened; even if I want to open up to someone, I can't. He saw it all happen and knows exactly what I went through. He told you everything, I am guessing.'

'I think so.'

'OK, now are we going to bed.'

'Yes, I'm shattered.'

***

The next day the team and the recruits went to the training centre that was out of the city, Will hadn't taken his team out there for months and he knew they could do with a good training session. He kept his team pretty fit and kept them sharp on the range, but this place was tough and he was hoping his team would be up to scratch so they could show the others how it was done. They all got out of the vehicles and gathered round the back of the truck.

'OK, what's going to happen is Alpha team will go through the building to my right here like a real call. They will clear the building, shoot the suspects and leave the hostages without a scratch. Bravo, you will watch and then it's your turn. You all got that?' They all nodded. 'Good, then let's get started.'

They played out scenarios through the morning in the handful of buildings. Alpha team first and then Bravo team followed suit. Alpha was pretty much on point and Stanson was learning fast. Bravo team were trying their best but were a little off the mark and made a few mistakes. But on the whole both Will and Kathy were happy with the teams and how they performed. They took a break and had some lunch and a drink, which was nice for them as it was often rushed when on call. Alpha was sitting separately to Bravo and only Stanson made an effort to speak among both teams. Kathy and Will watched them.

'These guys need to start talking and working together if they are ever going to work together properly.'

'Yeah, they are. What's your plan?'

'The assault course, we mix and match them to get them working together.'

'OK, then are you running it too?' Kathy asked.

'I think I will sit this one out actually.'

'Turning down an opportunity to show off that you are better than the rest. Wow, Will, you are growing up,' she said jokingly.

'Very funny. Now shall we get them in teams?'

They divided the teams into twos; in each was one Alpha and one Bravo member. They set them off round the course at five-minute intervals and then headed down to the finish to see what times they made. Will actually had five stop watches with him, colour coordinated for his team's call signs. They were waiting at the finish line, and Will turned to Kathy.

'This was a good idea getting the teams out here today.'

'Yeah, it's been fun.'

Just moments later the teams started to come through the finish and they all sat and had a drink while they waited for others to finish and for Will to work out who was fastest.

'OK, guys, we have some good times here so well done, everyone, but the fastest team were the Green team. Well done, Tom, good work. Second was Orange, so that is great from our Alpha rookie, Stanson. You other three teams were within ten seconds so don't feel too bad; you all did amazing. Now, Alpha, we have sniper training to do and, Bravo, it's back to building clearing.'

After another two hours of training, they were all done and were packing up the truck with the weapons.

'Stanson, good work on the sniper range today; you will get the hang of it in time. It's a big step when you have to take into account so many other factors. We can come out here a few times till you have passed the quals to work on a sniper call. We don't get too many but we do get them.'

'Thanks, Sergeant, I will study for the next time we come out here. It's new to me but I want to get better.'

'Good, now let's get back because I am ready to go home.'

***

Over the next couple of days, Will and Kathy were extremely busy: training, call outs and masses of paperwork to do. Saturday night had finally arrived and the team were all looking forward to Will's barbeque. It was around seven p.m. when Harvey arrived with Selena. Tom and Lynne had already been there for an hour, setting up.

'Wow, look at this place,' said Selena as they walked through the door.

Harvey just looked around, mouth open. They started to walk through the living area.

'You OK there, Harvey?' said Will as he met them, and showed them down the corridor to the roof terrace.

'Yeah, I just can't believe this is where you live.'

'It was my parents' place; I inherited it six years ago.'

'Only six years ago, Will,' Selena said. 'That's too long for me to be only just getting an invite.'

'Selena, honey.'

'No, it's OK, she is quite right. We have worked together for years and I should have had you round before, and I'm glad you are both here now. Grab a drink and some food. Palmer and Bennett are on their way up.'

Jimmy showed Bennett and Palmer up like he had Harvey. He opened the door for them, just as Will was walking back through.

'Holy shit, Sergeant, this place is yours?'

'Yes, Bennett, it's mine.'

'You must be seriously loaded. No wonder you know all those classy ladies.'

'This was my parents' place. I got it when they died. Yeah, they were wealthy though, and yes, it's how I got to meet all the women.'

They walked through to the roof terrace. They all greeted each other and started chatting. Will was talking to the guys when Kathy appeared. She was casually dressed but looked amazing; Will couldn't take his eyes off her. She went and got a drink, then she went over to Lynne and Selena who were looking at the view of the park.

'I am still in shock by this place and I can't believe my best friend didn't tell me.'

'Selena, you know I couldn't.'

'Yeah, I know.' She smiled. 'I am just jealous I was the last to know, but you would never even believe this side of him anyway from what Dan says. I mean, all I hear is how hard he works, how seriously he takes his job. Dan loves being on the team but I know how hard they have to work to stay on it. If his parents were this wealthy, he could have taken the easy way out, but he didn't.'

'You know, before his parents died he lived in an apartment not far from us. It was nice but it was just a small two-bed. I remember when I first met him like it was yesterday. Tom valued his opinion of me so much, probably more than that of his parents.' Lynne paused, smiling. 'He didn't tell me he had money till I married

Tom and we had been together five years at that point but he said he needed to be sure it would last before he trusted me.'

'I guess he's just a working guy with a healthy bank balance, that's nice.'

'So, Kathy, will you be moving in here soon?' Lynne asked.

'I have stayed over for the last week.'

'Well, with Will's age he will be popping the question soon enough. He's never mentioned kids but he won't want to wait long, I don't think,' Selena stated.

'I'm sorry.'

'Well that's how they are, Kathy. You know that surely,' Lynne added.

'We have only just got back together: I'm sure he won't be in a rush.'

The conversation moved on. They all ate and drank plenty and everyone was relaxed, all having an amazing evening. Will stood and shouted.

'OK, everyone.' They all fell silent. 'I just wanted to say thanks to you all for coming. I know it's taken too long to invite you here. You have had my back for a while now, some longer than others. I don't talk about my life much at the PD because they say money changes people and I have had people's opinion of me change when they find out. I am hoping though nothing will change after tonight and we will be the awesome team we always have been because loyalty in this game is what matters. Now, Kathy, if you want to come here please, because you are the woman that changed things and are responsible for tonight.' Kathy moved forward and stood next to Will, smiling at him. 'So, as our friends here are witnesses, I want to say thank you, that I love you, I never want to lose you. Now I know we have only been back together for a short time but,' he pulled out a ring box, 'I know I want to be with you forever. Will you marry me?'

Kathy froze. She stared at the ring then at Will with a look of pure shock on her face, then, without saying a word, she ran inside as quickly as she could. Lynne and Selena followed her, and Will watched them go. Tom walked over as the others sat in silence, not knowing what to say.

'It was too soon; I knew it was.'

'No, she was just surprised, that's all. I'm sure it's fine.'

'Maybe I should go and talk to her.'

'Yeah, I reckon you should.'

Will walked inside, down the corridor and looked for Kathy as he went. He found her talking with Lynne and Selena in the kitchen. Kathy had a coffee in her hands. When they saw Will coming, Selena and Lynne went back outside.

'So, do you want to tell me what just happened?' He stayed a little away from her and leaned on the kitchen top opposite her.

'You just asked me to marry you after being on and off for like four or five months.'

'I know that. I love you and I know I don't want to be with anyone else.'

'Yes, but what about me?'

'I don't understand.'

'Well, I just got my team who are about to qualify, I have only just begun and I can't take time off now.'

'Time off, now you really have lost me.'

'Well, you will want to get married soon and then have kids and all that means I will have to take time off work at least for a while.'

'What?'

'What do you mean, what?'

'Well, for one thing I only just asked you, and I personally was thinking a long engagement, maybe two years or so, and kids, I've not even thought that far ahead. All I wanted to do was promise that I was yours for life, if you will have me, but I guess that didn't come across properly.'

'Really?' Kathy smiled.

'Yes, really.'

Kathy put down the cup and moved forward to him, wrapping her arms around him. He held her tightly for a moment and kissed the top of her head. She looked up at him.

'Then, yes, I accept your promise. I will marry you.'

He got the ring out of his pocket and put it on her finger. Then they went back outside to be with their friends.

Chapter 19

Late Monday afternoon, Kathy was in her office, waiting for news on her team. She had decided against observing because she was so nervous and didn't think she could sit and watch without saying anything. Will and his team were out on a call and there had been quite a few so she had spent most of the day on her own, waiting. She went to get a coffee and Captain Bridge came in back from the assessments.

'Sergeant Hill, have to say your team and Stanson were very impressive today. They all passed with flying colours, so as of tomorrow they are on shift.'

Captain Bridge walked across the squad office, into his own and closed the door. Just then her team came in with Stanson, all laughing and smiling.

'Hey, guys, well done, the captain just told me, fantastic news.'

'Thanks, Sergeant, it was really tough but we got through.'

They were all sitting around talking and drinking coffee, when Will and his team came back in.

'Well, Stanson, are you Alpha or not?'

'Yes, Sergeant, I am.'

'Well done, now the hard work really starts. Now follow me to my office.'

He was taken aback but followed Will, shut the door behind him and sat down.

'OK, so as of tomorrow you are full time on my team, so let's go over a few ground rules. Never be late for shift unless I know you will be. Never show up drunk or hung over. Never disobey an order of mine and always listen to instructions and ask if you are unsure of anything.'

'OK, Sergeant, no worries, I won't let you down.'

'OK, well, that's today done so let's go and have a drink to celebrate.'

Both teams met up at Charlie's. They were the only ones in there, but more than made up for the lack of people in there. They took up three tables down near the pool table.

'Now, everyone,' Will said. 'The first round is on me, then you are all on soda, because I don't want anyone drunk or hung over on their first shift, because I will be checking, if I think there is the slightest chance you are.'

Will and Kathy took note of what they all wanted and went to the bar to get the drinks.

'Is he serious?' Blain laughed.

'Oh yeah, he's serious,' Bennett replied, 'has a breathalyser in his office and everything. Seen him use it a few times.'

'Wow, really? That's harsh.'

'Not for Sergeant Falco, you'll see,' Harvey said. 'You have no idea what he expects.'

'But we are on Sergeant Hill's team,' Walker stated.

'Yeah, but you guys are Bravo, so any job we get called together Falco has point, always does.'

'How bad can it be though?'

Will's team looked at each other and laughed, including Tom.

'Let's put it this way, after your first call with Alpha and Falco, you will be glad you aren't Stanson.'

'So why are you all still there?'

'Because he's the best, and I wouldn't have him any other way,' Harvey continued. 'He is a hard ass but I am better for working with him. Most SWAT officers have worked with him but can't hack it but I don't know anyone I would rather have my back.'

'True story,' Bennett joined in. 'Now, Sergeant Hill is good too. She was Alpha till she passed her Sergeants, but Falco, he is the ultimate.'

Will and Kathy walked back over to the tables with the drinks. The teams suddenly went silent.

'What's going on?'

'Nothing, Falco, just talking,' Tom replied.

'About me I'm guessing.'

'Yeah, just letting everyone know what they are in for tomorrow.'

'Don't scare them. I was building them up to that,' Kathy joked.

'Hey, I'm not that bad.'

'Yes, you are,' Kathy replied. 'I remember my first shift on Alpha team. I was so nervous and you wouldn't let me do anything, but it got better eventually. I just hope our first day is quiet, build them up to you on a bad day.'

'Wow, thanks, sweet heart, love you too.'

The teams talked, laughed and joked and got to know each other for a few hours. Will saw it was getting late so he and Kathy called it a night and reminded everyone not to be late in the next morning.

***

Will arrived and was getting coffee for him and Kathy when the teams walked into the office. He was impressed that they were all on time and no one seemed to be hung over. He took the coffees into Kathy's office and sat on the edge of the desk, putting hers down and having a drink of his own.

'So, are you ready?'

'Of course.'

'You know I'm here if you need me.'

'I know, I'm hoping our first call is with you. No matter what I said last night, show them how it's done and all that.'

'Jumping in the deep end works well too, you know.'

'Well, whatever it is I'm sure they will be fine.'

Will had another drink of his coffee and his beeper went off.

'Seriously, I can't even finish my coffee.' He stood up. 'See you soon.'

'Yeah, you will.'

He left followed by his team. Kathy sat back in her chair and took a deep breath; she knew today was going to be a tough day.

***

They pulled up inside the cordon. Will got out of the truck and headed over to the lieutenant that was there, organising the officers. It seemed to be quite chaotic, officers running around; nothing seemed to be organised.

'Sergeant, we're glad you are here. We have an unknown number of assailants in that department store. They have an unknown number of hostages but we don't know where they are.'

'So, a big building with what, four or five floors and they could be anywhere?'

'That's about right.'

'Well, in that case we are going to need more officers; my team can't cover that alone quick enough.'

'We have plenty you can use.'

'No, it's OK, I know some.'

Will walked over to the truck.

'Control, this is Alpha team; we are going to need Bravo team down here and let Lieutenant Planter know that this is a major incident and have another team on standby.'

'Received, Alpha team.'

Will turned to the team.

'This is going to be a tough one, guys. We all need to be prepared for literally anything. We need to wait for Bravo team. They don't even know where these guys are with a lot of hostages.'

Lieutenant Planter and Bravo team arrived but Kathy wasn't with them.

'Where's Sergeant Hill?'

'She had to go and do something, Sergeant, so we got told to come and report to you,' Fremont replied.

'OK, that changes things.'

Will went and had a conversation with Lieutenant Planter. They looked at the floor plans and worked out how they were going to work it. Will hated such large buildings with so many uncertainties; it's how officers got hurt or killed, if it wasn't planned right, and he had seen it happen. When they were organised, he went back to the teams.

'OK, listen up. So, Stanson, you take Fremont as Orange team. Tom, take Ford and Blain as Green. Bennett, take Walker as White team. Palmer, you and Webb will be Yellow. Harvey, you are with me. This is going to be tough; we don't have a confirmed number of suspects so we go floor by floor. Yellow team, after the ground floor you will secure the stairwell. The elevators are off, as are the escalators. We clear a floor at a time. Don't stop to help the injured if you come across any as we don't have time for that. Be quick but be right. Watch your partners. Let's all get out in one piece, shall we?'

The teams went in, they spread out across the floor. They cleared the first two floors with relative ease. On the second floor there were two assailants by the escalators; Stanson took one and Will the other. Shots were fired down from the floor above so White team secured the escalators and took down two more shooters. They moved up to the third floor when Will realised there was only one floor left and that must be where they all were.

Up on the top floor, the suspects had got all the hostages sitting on the floor. Many were huddled in groups, especially the families. A man was walking around them. He was observing them all as he went, and it became clear he was looking for someone.

'Marcus.' One of the others came over to him. 'The police are here and SWAT are inside. If they carry on at this speed they will be up here in no time. This is taking too long.'

'OK.' He turned to the hostages. 'Mrs Cheetham, we know you are here, and if I have to shoot every hostage in here till you step forward I will, because your husband is in serious trouble and owes my boss a lot of money. So, we are going to collect one way or another.'

No one stood up. He walked around the hostages again. There was a group of wealthy ladies all together. They were all looking down. He noticed and started walking around towards them.

On the floor below, White team stayed at the escalators once more to stop the escape of any of the suspects. Green team stayed on the third floor too; they would go up when they heard Will announce. The others moved up the stairwell. When they got to the top, Will instructed them all how to move in and where to go.

Will opened the door a fraction; they weren't far away and he could see a large number of hostages and seven suspects.

'Marcus, I'm telling you SWAT are on their way to this floor; I just spotted them at the bottom of the escalators. They just shot Bill and his mate, probably got the others too. We need to go.'

'Not without the one I came for. So, Mrs Cheetham if you don't come forward, I am going to shoot this child.' He pointed his gun at a very young girl. Will was ready to move when a woman stood up.

'I'm Mrs Cheetham.'

Will recognised her; it was his ex-fiancée.

'OK, if you would like to come with me. We have to go. It seems my men couldn't hold off the police as long as I would have liked.'

At that point Will opened the door and moved forward with Harvey behind him.

'NYPD, drop your weapons,' Will announced.

Stanson and Fremont broke off and came around and covered other suspects, and Tom, Ford and Blain came up the escalator and covered the rest, who all pointed their guns back at the teams.

'I don't think so,' Marcus said. 'Me and this woman are leaving and you will move out of the way because I have no issue shooting anyone in this room.' He had her right in front of him, moving backwards.

'You are not leaving here unless in cuffs or a body bag.'

'Well, how are you going to do that when you can't get a clear shot?'

'Well, you shouldn't rely on using a hostage as a shield; you never know when they will stumble.' He winked at his ex.

Suddenly she did exactly that; she faked a stumble in her high heels. She gave Will enough of a view to get a shot off and hit him. He fell to the floor. His men all then put their weapons down as Will took aim at another one of them.

'Control, this is Alpha team; we are all clear.'

'Received, Alpha team. We have PD on their way in now.'

Will started to make his way to the stairs. He didn't want to hang around, and Tom nodded at him to leave the scene. His ex-fiancée saw him leaving and stopped him. She was a well-dressed woman about five foot eleven. She had shoulder-length blonde hair and her overall appearance was pristine.

'Will, long time no see, thanks for stopping them.'

'Just doing my job.'

'You were always good at it, and I know you enjoy it too. That's why you wouldn't give it up.'

'You married your millionaire, I see.'

'Ah yes, I did, four years now.'

'Good, I'm happy for you.'

'Really, after the way we split up?'

'Yeah, Carla, I am. I have moved on from that now and I realised a long time ago it just wasn't meant to be.'

'Really? I heard it took quite a few women to get over me.'

'They weren't to get over you, and I am done with all that now; I just got engaged.'

'Wow, congratulations. Do I know her?'

'I doubt it, she works on SWAT.'

'Oh, is she here now?' She looked round at the others.

'No, she is on something else.'

'I honestly thought you would marry into money. I know it's what your parents wanted for you, and women with careers don't tend to want children and I can see you having plenty of those.' She touched his arm in an affectionate way.

'My parents wanted me to be happy and I am very happy, thanks. Now, I have to get back to work if you will excuse me.'

'Well, it was great seeing you, Will. Take care. I should call my husband anyway.'

Will went down the stairs and out. He wanted to get back as soon as possible. He wanted to find out why Kathy had missed such a big shout.

Chapter 20

Will got back to the office, poured himself a coffee and looked into Kathy's office. She wasn't there, so he walked over to the captain's office to ask where she was. He knew Kathy would have cleared her absence with him.

'Captain, have you seen Sergeant Hill?'

'Yes, she had to go out.'

'Do you know where?'

'Yes, I do, she won't be long.'

Will stepped into the office and closed the door.

'Where is she?'

'Falco, she will be back anytime and then you will find out.'

'I'm not allowed to know? I don't understand.'

'You are being kept in the dark for good reason, Sergeant.'

'I had to cover a major incident with both Alpha and Bravo teams, and she is my girlfriend, so I think that qualifies me to know, Captain. '

'She didn't want you to know, not until a few things were worked out. Hence why she went when you got called out.'

'So, she said not to tell me?'

'Yes, because she like me knows you will over react.'

'Well, let me tell you not knowing right now is having a similar effect. Now will you please tell me what the hell is going on?' Will shouted.

Just then there was a knock at the door and a man they didn't know came in. He was wearing a grey suit with a tie; he was not too tall, only about five foot eight and he was quite slim. He had light brown hair.

'I can explain that for you, Sergeant,' he said.

He closed the door and came right into the office so he was standing by the captain's desk. He turned and faced Will and gestured for him to sit down. Will sat.

'And who the hell are you?'

'I'm Detective Park, from the major case squad, just transferred to New York. I have been talking to Sergeant Hill this morning.'

'OK, where is she?'

'She will be back within the next hour, but I need to speak to you.'

'What about?'

'Well Sergeant Hill has been getting some calls and messages from an unknown number. She also got sent some photos of an intimate nature. It appears someone has been stalking her.'

'What? She has a stalker and no one thought to tell me about this?'

'She wanted it to be investigated first. It started when the two of you weren't together, and we have been in touch with her since then, but we don't think it's a simple stalking case.'

'Sounds simple enough to me. I can't believe she didn't tell me about this!' Will shouted.

'Sergeant, she wanted it looking into before she told you and expressed to us from the start that it wasn't to be discussed with you until now.'

'I can't believe this; I get criticised for keeping secrets and then she does this.' He was furious and got up and walked out, slamming the door behind him.

'Where's he gone? I wasn't actually done,' Detective Park asked Captain Bridge, looking very confused.

'Where he always goes, the gym. He goes down there when he is mad or stressed.'

'Does he do that a lot?'

'Better that than some of the things he could do.'

'Has he never thought of talking to a shrink?'

'Not Falco, he would rather hit something.'

Detective Park walked down to the gym and, sure enough, Will was there taking out his frustration on the punch bag. He was angry this had been kept from him. He knew he kept secrets but this was different.

'Captain Bridge said I would find you here.'

'Yeah so? What do you want now?'

'I hadn't actually finished upstairs. There is more to the stalker than I managed to tell you before you walked out.'

Will stopped and looked at him.

'What do you mean more?'

'Well, although the stalker was contacting Sergeant Hill, we don't think she was the target.'

'I don't get it, why would someone stalk her then?'

'Look at these pictures.'

Detective Park showed him pictures of Kathy and Stanson, him and Kathy and Kathy going into Tom's house. Then he showed him one of him and Ashleigh.

'Now look at this.'

He handed Will a note; he read it.

So, you have had three out of six in Alpha team. You really are a whore. You don't deserve Will Falco. He should be with someone like Ashleigh or better still me. End it or I will!!!!!!!

'What the hell is this?'

'She got that with the photos, but this confirms what we think. Sergeant Hill isn't the target. You are.

***

Will went back upstairs, he got a coffee and went in the captain's office, closing the door behind them. Will had calmed down and decided to listen to what the detective had to say. He was completely lost with what was going on.

'I don't get how I'm the target, who would target me?' He paused for a moment, remembering his conversation with Mr X. Could this be what he had meant?

'It will be someone who knows you, possibly for a while, and they have been watching Kathy and you for a number of weeks. Your job makes it hard to get to you so they went through Sergeant Hill.'

'Kathy has the same job.'

'But as a female, one who has been recently injured, she could be seen as more vulnerable, and you had separated so maybe they saw that as a weakness, but you got back together so they sent the pictures probably to try and cause a divide again, and they must know you well enough to know exactly what buttons to push.'

'Well, there isn't many on that list.'

'There has to be someone, maybe someone who doesn't stand out to you, but until we work this out, we want a detective with you at all times.'

'Please tell me you are kidding.'

'No, why?'

'Detective, every time you lot have an armed suspect, you call us, so how are you going to protect me?'

'At least let me have a detective stay with you and let me put someone on your home. We need to look out for any unusual activity.'

'OK, you can put someone outside my place, inside is perfectly safe.'

'Where do you live? I will send them straight there.'

'There,' Will replied, pointing to the picture of him and Ashleigh.

'Really, Park Avenue, we thought that was her place.'

'No, her parents live a few blocks away, but she lives off the island now.' He paused and looked at Park. 'Before you ask, it was my parents' place. They were killed, so it's mine now.'

'I wasn't going to ask.'

Just then Will saw Kathy come back in the office. He left and walked over to her, took her hand and went in his office. He sat on the desk. She closed the door and stood in front of him.

'Will, I'm sorry.'

'I can't believe you didn't say anything about this.'

'I didn't want to worry you till I knew what this was. We weren't together when it started and when we got back together it stopped for a while. Then I got the photos so I knew it wasn't as simple as I thought it was.'

'You should have told me. Instead I find out from some detective I don't even know.'

'Will, he's a good guy, and has been really helpful through this.'

'So, like Stanson you expect me to trust someone with my life that I don't know.'

'Will, you need to let this guy in or we may never find out who this person is and that could be a dangerous decision to make.'

'You think I need this guy to protect me? Are you serious?'

'Not protect you, Will, but he is trained in this sort of thing and may be able to find this person before they get to you.'

Will sighed and looked at her. He knew she was worried on this and that made him wonder if this was as serious as everyone else was thinking it was.

'I was so worried when you didn't show for such a big call out, and you had all this going on. No more secrets, OK?'

'Yeah, I promise and sorry about that call out. I wanted to go while you were out, but when they called Bravo, I was already there. How did it go?'

'Not bad, your team can follow orders so that's a good start.'

'Good, I'm glad they did so well.'

Will took hold of her hands and pulled her a little closer.

'So, how are you?'

'I'm OK, a bit shocked by all this but generally good.'

'I know it's crazy, some mad person after me,' he half joked.

She looked at him and she could tell that the anger was covering up his concern about this.

'You're worried about this, aren't you?'

'Not worried really but I hate not knowing what I'm up against. Normally on a call I know what I'm facing and I handle it, but this is different. They are staying hidden and trying to get to me in a completely different way. I'm not used to that.'

Just then Detective Park opened the door.

'Sorry to interrupt, Sergeant, but where are we on the detective sticking with you?'

'All right, I will agree to it on two conditions: first, it's you because I don't like most of your lot, and second, don't get in my way.'

'I will have to check I can do it.'

'OK, but you may want to hurry up. Who knows when our beepers will go off.'

Detective Park nodded and closed the door.

'You are letting him shadow you? You do think this is serious.'

'Like you say, if I don't let him in how do we catch them and I'm covering all angles, and it's not just about me, is it?'

He kissed her and held her tight. Just then their beepers went off.

'Do they know when we are having a moment or something?'

'Must do.'

They walked out of his office to meet Lieutenant Planter.

'We have a man shooting up Times Square. Alpha, Bravo and Delta to attend. Sergeant Falco, it's your call. One officer has been shot so let's take it easy with this one.'

'Sure thing, Lieutenant. Are you coming?' Will shouted to Park. He nodded. 'Then come on, we have to move.'

***

The teams arrived with Lieutenant Planter. He got the information from the senior officer there and briefed Will, Kathy and Price.

'OK, this guy is firing at anyone who shows their face. He has multiple weapons and has already shot one officer in the leg. Sergeant Falco, what's your play?'

'Alpha team, go at him from this side. Bravo, make your way round and come at him from behind and be quick to get in place. If we can't take him you can while he is focussed on us. Delta, cover the top end and the PD cover the other but keep them well back because if he isn't scared to shoot them it could get messy.'

'Sounds good, Sergeant, get it done and get him off the streets.'

'OK, Price, Hill, get your teams into position. Let me know when you are there.'

Kathy and Price took their teams and explained as they went.

'OK, Harvey with me, Tom and Palmer, go one street left, Bennett and Stanson, go one street right, OK?'

They all nodded and they all set off, but Tom hung back and stopped him.

'Does this remind you of last week?'

'Yeah, a little now you mention it, but it has one big difference and that's this guy likes to shoot at people.'

Detective Park walked over to Will.

'You can stay here,' Will said before he spoke.

'I can't do my job from here, Sergeant.'

'And I can't do mine if you get in the way, that was the deal.'

When they were all in place, Will edged down the street to the end to get a look at the suspect. He wasn't that far away and he stood looking around. He was only young, early twenties, Will estimated. He was around five foot seven with scruffy brown hair and a short beard. Will stepped back before he was seen.

'OK, he's got a semi-automatic and a handgun plus another one tucked in his belt, so let's not rush this,' he said to Harvey.

Will looked again. The suspect was looking at his phone. Will made a quick decision and took a chance to catch him off guard; he broke cover. Suddenly the suspect looked up and turned in his direction and fired. Will fired one back and the suspect was down. Will stepped back and leaned against the wall.

'The suspect is down, but we need EMTs now; Sergeant Falco is hit.'

Chapter 21

'Repeat your last message, Harvey,' Tom radioed.

'Sergeant Falco is hit,' Harvey replied.

'OK, Bennett and Stanson secure the suspect. Bravo team secure the scene. Harvey I'm coming to you.'

Tom ran down to Will's position, followed by Palmer. Will was now sitting on the floor, weapon and gear next to him.

'You OK? Where are you hit?' Tom crouched in front of him.

'He just caught my arm.'

Will was holding it. The EMTs arrived. He moved his hand. There was quite a lot of blood. EMTs started to assess the wound.

'This is quite deep. We will have to take you in for stitches.'

'Really?'

'Yes really, we can't just bandage this up.'

'Will, you need to go and get that sorted properly; it looks really bad.'

'Yeah OK.' He looked up at Tom who had stood up. 'Just let Kathy know I'm OK.'

'I will do that now.' He walked off to find her.

The EMTs helped Will stand, and walked him slowly to the ambulance. Harvey collected his gear and took it to the truck. Detective Park was waiting for him by the ambulance.

'Think you are safe now, Sergeant?'

'You think this is connected?' Will said, sitting down on the back step.

'Don't you?'

'Well, if it was him, he won't be doing it again.'

'He's dead?'

'Yeah, that's what I do when people shoot me.'

'He shot you in the arm and you still shot him.'

'Yeah, of course I did.'

'Right, well, who can we take with us for an armed guard?'

'I'm sorry?'

'Well, evidence suggests the person orchestrating this is a woman, so you need a guard, especially now.'

'I thought that was you.'

'I think we need to step it up. I mean, you are the best shot in the city and they still got you.'

'Well, we can't have one of mine, Tom needs them. Ask Kathy, see if she can spare one.'

'OK, don't go just yet,' he said to the EMT as he ran off.

On the square, Bennett and Stanson stood with the suspect.

'Sergeant Falco managed to hit him, perfect shot to the head, after he was shot. I'm telling you that guy is not normal,' Bennett said, looking at the suspect.

'How so?'

'His aim is so perfect. Most of the PD could never shoot like that on a good day, never mind after being shot in the arm.'

'I guess so,' Stanson said, looking around. He saw Richards just down the block, hovering round. She dropped what looked like a cell phone into a trash can, then walked off.

'Did you see that?'

'What?'

'Richards just put a cell phone in that trash can.'

'Are you sure it wasn't trash?'

'I don't think so. Let me go and look.'

'OK, but be quick, we are supposed to be staying with the suspect till the coroner gets here.'

As Stanson walked over, Delta team got another call out. He paused to make sure she wasn't still around. Stanson moved a piece of paper and there it was: a cell phone. He took out a tissue and picked it up. He took it over to Bennett.

'It is a phone, a burner by the look of it.'

'So, what?'

'Don't you think it's a bit weird.'

'Yeah, but she is really odd. Is it on?'

'Yeah, it is.' Stanson started looking through the phone. 'Holy shit, she sent a message to another phone with Sergeant Falco's exact location on it, where he was shot.'

'Does this guy have a phone?'

They both searched him, keeping an eye out as they did so.

'Here it is.'

'Look at the messages.'

'Yeah, it's here, look,' Bennett said, showing Stanson the message. 'We have to tell someone.'

'What about that detective that was with Sergeant Falco; he came with us.'

'Why him? He's not SWAT.'

'I saw him with the Sergeant earlier back at the office and he spoke to Sergeant Hill too. He's following Falco for a reason and if the sergeant trusts him maybe we should too. It could all be connected.'

'OK. you take them to him later after shift. Don't let them out of your sight till then and don't say anything to anyone because we don't want Richards trying to deny this or covering it up somehow. If she did this, we need to make sure she is done for it or maybe there is a perfectly good reason for it.'

'OK, so we don't tell Tom or Sergeant Hill?'

'No, just in case someone overhears us and Richards finds out. Take them to him only.'

'OK, will do.'

***

At the hospital Will was in a private room having his wound sewn up. Park was sitting in the room with him and Fremont was stood outside the door.

'So how long will this take?' Will asked the nurse.

'Well, when I'm done, the doctor will come and check on you, but he will probably want to keep you in overnight.'

'I don't think so.'

'Why not?' asked Park.

'Because I hate hospitals.'

'It's not so bad, private room, armed guard.'

'I would rather be at home.'

'Well, I will speak to the doctor when I'm done,' the nurse said.

'So, Sergeant, have you thought any more about who this could be?'

'I have no idea, I told you that.'

'No one hates you that much?'

'I don't think so, not women anyway.'

'No exs?'

'I saw my ex-fiancée today but she is happily married to a millionaire.'

'Any others?'

'Nothing serious, and I stay friends with most of the women I sleep with.'

'How the hell do you manage that?'

'I guess I just treat them well.'

'OK, Sergeant, I'm done; I will get the doctor for you,' the nurse said as she left.

Will started to get up so he could get ready to leave.

'What, you can't sit and wait for the doctor?'

'I'm not allowed to stand up now, Detective?'

'You just got shot. You are not invincible. Someone is after you. It's OK to sit and relax for five minutes.'

'What did Kathy say this morning?'

'Why do you ask that?'

'Because that's something she would say.'

'Well, let's just say she is worried about you, that you are all work, that you never take time off, and that you will go after this person, whoever it is, no matter what.'

'She said all that?'

'Yeah, she did.'

'OK, I will sit and wait.'

'You really love her.'

'Yeah.'

'I can tell by the way you respect her opinion like that. You both entrusted me to work this out and I promise I will, whatever it takes.'

Will sat thinking for a few moments and his conversation with Mr X came back to mind.

'Hang on a minute, the other week I went to see Mr X in prison.'

'Mr X?'

'Yeah, he killed my parents and is the one that kidnapped and shot Kathy. Part of his deal to plead guilty was that I went to speak with him.'

'You think he has something to do with this?'

'No, he's more just the walk over and shoot you type of guy, but he said that someone was coming after me. I thought nothing of it till today. He knew about this, but I have no idea how.'

'Well, we will look at all his contacts and try and figure out what he meant. If he knows something, we will find out what.'

'He won't tell you if you ask him though. He made that clear when I spoke to him. You will have to find his contact and ask them.'

***

After the doctor had seen Will, he signed himself out, sent Fremont back to the office and Park drove him home.

'So, Sergeant, let me know what you are doing tomorrow. You have two guys outside, but if your building is as secure as you say, I'm sure you won't need them.'

Will sat for a moment before he got out and looked at Park. Maybe Kathy was right. Maybe he would have to let him in just a little, to help him catch whoever was after him.

'I can't believe I'm going to say this because I really don't like people knowing my business, but do you want to look inside and check it out. Kathy will be back anytime, might help with the case.'

'OK, sure, it may help get inside their head.'

They parked the car and went inside.

'This is Jimmy he works most days.'

'Hi, Jimmy, I'm Detective Park. Has anyone been asking about Sergeant Falco lately?'

'Not me, but Charles, the night guy, said a guy stopped him the other morning as he left, asking if Sergeant Falco was at home.'

'What did Charles say?'

'We use protocol. If they won't leave a name or they speak to us outside, Sergeant Falco isn't home.'

'OK.'

'If they are legit, they would come in and the cameras would pick them up. Are you OK, Will?' Jimmy asked, pointing to Will's arm.

'Yes, I'm fine, line of duty and all that.'

'OK, if you need anything just call down.'

'Kathy will be here soon, so can you let her up? She has forgotten her code.'

'Yes, of course.'

They walked to the elevator.

'Let her up?'

'Yeah, it's a secure elevator and you need a code to get upstairs. She has forgotten the code so I need to create her one that she remembers.'

'The door staff have it though.'

'They have a different code to me so it rings a bell upstairs when they use theirs.'

'Really, that's high tech.'

'Yeah, but security at its best.'

They travelled up the elevator in silence, Park unsure of what to expect. Sergeant Falco had been described as a mystery down in his office, but he seemed really open with him, almost trusting, and he wondered why. They got to the top floor and Will opened the door.

'Go and take a look around. You will see it's perfectly safe.'

'Wow, this is impressive.'

'Like I told you, it was my parents' place. I grew up here and moved back in when they died.'

'They were wealthy?'

'Yeah, very.'

'So why the force, why SWAT?'

'I met Tom when we were kids; his dad was a cop. My dad believed in being the best at whatever you did, so with his help I trained and worked hard. He supported me all the way, and they were so pleased when I joined SWAT and when I took over Alpha team.'

'That's great. My parents hate me being a cop.'

'Why's that?'

'They don't think it's a suitable career.'

'So why do it?'

'Because I wanted to help people and med school was a bit too much for me.'

'Where are you from?'

'Miami, but I needed a change so when the job came up here, I went for it.'

'OK, well, take a look around. I'm going to get a drink'

Just then a beeping noise sounded.

'That's Kathy on her way up.'

'Well, I will make this quick then.'

Park went down the corridor, checking each room as he went. Will went to the door and let Kathy in.

'Oh my god, Will, why are you here? Did the doctor say you could be?'

'Not really but I prefer to be at home.'

'So are you OK?' she said, gesturing at his bandaged arm.

'Yeah, they stitched it up. It's sore but I have painkillers.'

'OK, but you worried the hell out of me.'

'I know.' He kissed her head. 'I'm going for a wash. Can you let Park out when he's done?'

'You let him up here?'

'You said I had to let him in to allow him to catch whoever is doing this.'

'I didn't think you would though.'

'I listen sometimes, you know, and after today whatever will help.'

Will had gone into his bedroom when Park came back through.

'Will said he will see you tomorrow.'

'Yeah OK, I think I am beginning to understand a few things.'

'I take it that's a good thing.'

'Yes very. Good night, Sergeant Hill.'

'I will call Jimmy and get him to let you down.'

'Thanks, it's definitely a secure place to live. He will be safe here.'

'Good night, Detective.'

***

Detective Park went back to his office to find Stanson waiting for him with the two phones in evidence bags he had picked up to preserve any evidence on them.

'Can I help you, Officer?'

'Yeah, I'm Officer Stanson. I'm on Sergeant Falco's team. I think I have something here.'

'What's that?'

'Two phones, one was on the man that shot the sergeant and the other Officer Richards put in a trash can. She sent a message to the suspect and told him where Sergeant Falco was, when he got shot.'

'Really, you saw her dump it?'

'Yeah, but no one else did.'

'Well, Stanson, thanks. Now do you have some time? I think we need to have a good look at Richards and what we see and discuss can't go any further.'

'OK, no problem, I just want to help. Only Bennett knows about the phone. We didn't say anything to anyone.'

'Good, we need to keep this quiet till we know more. Richards may be innocent, she may be the one organising it all, but till we know we can't say anything.'

Chapter 22

The next morning Kathy was getting ready, when Will woke up. He looked at the clock and got up quickly.

'Why didn't you wake me?'

'You're not going in today; you need to rest.'

'Come on, I'm fine. I can go in and do some paperwork, training records and other bits.'

'Will, you can barely move your arm; you were shot and need to rest.'

'I will be resting, just at my desk.'

'I'm not going to win, am I?'

'No, and I want to keep an eye on things.'

'OK, get ready quickly then. We need to get a cab, as you are obviously unable to ride in today.'

'OK, but can you help me get my shirt on?'

'Really, but you can work?'

'Once I'm dressed, yes.'

Kathy went around the bed and helped him with his uniform. He sat on the bed so she could reach. When he put his arm in, it was obvious he was in pain. Kathy looked at him in a way he knew what she was thinking.

'Honestly, I'm good.'

'Come on then, let's go, because we will be late.'

'OK, I'm coming.'

When they got downstairs Charles was working; he was always on when Will went to work. Will had called down before he went to bed to organise a car for work.

'Your car has just arrived.'

'Thanks, Charles.'

'A car?'

'Yeah, you can never get a cab at this time of day.'

They went out and got in the black town car that was waiting for them.

'Well, this is nice.'

'I use these when I need to. Don't get used to it because as soon as my arm is healed, I will be back on two wheels.'

'Yeah, I know, but I can enjoy this, can't I?'

They travelled the rest of the way in quiet. Kathy kept looking at Will. She knew he shouldn't be going in today but she also knew she wouldn't get her way on this; he was stubborn. Will was in pain but he also knew if he went in, he could work on what was going on. He could get Park to come over so they could try and narrow down who would do this. He was starting to feel a bit off it too, even felt a bit warm, but he hated admitting that this had taken its toll on him; he prided himself on his fitness and health. When they arrived at the office, the teams hadn't got in yet, but he could see Park in the captain's office; at least that saved a phone call. Kathy made the coffees and took them into his office. He followed and shut the door behind them. He put his arms around her and she turned to face him.

'Sergeant Falco, this is not how to behave in the office.'

'I don't care, I need some TLC.' He kissed her. She let him for a moment then pulled away as she heard the others arrive.

'I have work to do.'

'You can do it in a minute.'

He was about to kiss her again when there was a knock on the door. Will opened it. Tom stood there looking confused.

'Wasn't expecting you today, Sergeant.'

'Well, I have a mountain of paperwork to do so I thought I would come and get it done.'

'How's the arm?'

'Painful but OK.'

Kathy squeezed past Tom and went across to her own office.

'I interrupted, didn't I?'

'Yeah, but you might as well come in.'

Tom stepped in and shut the door. Will went around the desk and sat down in his chair and had a drink of coffee.

'So, are you going to catch me up?'

'With what?'

Tom sat opposite Will. With the chaos of yesterday, he hadn't had a chance to find out what was going on.

'The detective shadowing you all of a sudden, you getting shot. I know it's something but this is the first time I have had a chance to ask you to find out.'

'OK, I will tell you, but it stays between us, OK?'

'Always you know that.'

Will explained everything that had happened the day before, all about the stalker and how they believed he was the target. Tom listened and was surprised by the whole thing.

'And you don't know who it is?'

'No, can't think of anyone.'

'But you think this is what Mr X was talking about?'

'Possibly, I don't know how he knew though.'

Will stood up and felt dizzy so sat back down straight away.

'You OK, Will?'

'Yeah, I just need a minute.'

'You don't look well; do you want me to get Kathy?'

'No, I'm fine honest, just stood up too fast.'

Tom's beeper went and he stood up.

'Wow, that must be weird for you.'

'No, it's OK, you best go and don't let these guys give you any hassle, OK?'

'I won't.'

Tom left. Will sat back in his chair and took a deep breath. Maybe he should have stayed at home. He was working through his paperwork when Captain Bridge came to his door.

'Sergeant Falco, what the hell are you doing here?'

'Paperwork, Captain. I haven't had much time to get it done this week.'

'You are allowed to take time off, you know, when you get shot, Sergeant. No one expects you to be here today.'

'So, I keep getting told, Captain. Honestly, I'm OK and I am staying here and just doing paperwork. Tom and Kathy have everything else covered.'

'Well, if you need to go home just go. We are just going over some things to see if we can get a lead on your stalker. We will let you know if we find anything.'

'Thanks, Captain.'

***

Will was going through his team's training records when he heard the teams come back in. He got up and went across the office to get another coffee. He hadn't wanted to eat anything so coffee was all that was keeping him going.

'How did it go, Tom?'

'Fine, Sergeant, wasn't really needed.'

Suddenly Will felt dizzy. He put his cup down and leaned on the desk.

'Sergeant, are you OK?'

Will collapsed on the floor, out cold.

'Will, shit, someone call an ambulance. Kathy!' Tom shouted.

Kathy came out of her office; she saw Will on the floor.

'What happened?'

'I don't know. He just collapsed.'

'OK, check his breathing and his pulse.'

The captain and Park came out to see what the commotion was.

'OK, everyone move back,' Captain Bridge ordered, crouching next to Will. 'Has someone called an ambulance?'

'Yes, Captain, they are on the way,' Harvey answered.

The few minutes it took for the ambulance to arrive felt like forever to Kathy. When the paramedics arrived, they checked him over quickly and got a drip in his arm, then got him on a stretcher. Harvey and Stanson helped them get him down the stairs.

'Detective, go with him. Fremont, you too, don't leave his side, understood?'

'Yes, Captain,' Fremont replied.

Park nodded and followed him out. Tom took Kathy into her office and sat her down. She was shaking, and was fighting back the tears.

'I'm so sorry.'

'For what, Tom?'

'Just before the call, Will stood up and had to sit back down. I should have said something.'

'Tom, it's not your fault. I should never have let him come in today, but you know Will, he is stubborn as hell. He was told to stay in the hospital last night and still came home.'

'He doesn't change, been like that since he joined the force, never takes a day off unless he has to.' He paused for a moment then looked right at her. 'Will told me about what's going on.'

'I thought he might.'

'We best get whoever did this.'

'We will and you know Will, he will be fine.'

Kathy really hoped she was right on both counts. These last couple of days had really scared her. It always seemed like Will was untouchable but this was the reality and now he was being rushed to hospital.

Chapter 23

At the hospital Will was taken into a room in the ER to find out what was wrong. Park and Fremont waited outside. Fremont stood at the door and Park was pacing up and down. He went to get a coffee for them both. They were taking a very long time. Nurses had come in and out of his room several times, with different trolleys holding different equipment. They had closed the blinds so no one could see into the room unless the door was open, and Park wondered if that was a bad thing or not. He had glanced in as the door had opened every time someone went in and they seemed to be very busy around him. A doctor came out and walked over to Park and Fremont.

'Are you with Sergeant Falco?'

'Yeah, what's going on?'

'He has a very serious infection in the gunshot wound he got yesterday. When the bullet hit his arm fragments of metal came away and went into the tissue. They can't be seen without an X-ray but because the bullet never got close to the bone, he didn't have one yesterday and the wound looked clean. We need to take him upstairs to the operating theatre to get the pieces out. We just don't have the equipment to see them down here. There are five in total and we need to get past the infected tissue first. Once he is done we will transfer him to a room and give him some very strong antibiotics.'

'That's what caused the infection? But it happened so fast, and is so bad, is that normal? I've never seen anything like this.'

'Yes, these pieces are dirty with gun powder residue and oil. I have seen two other cases just like this one but they didn't make it. The pieces of metal lodged in the heart in both cases and we couldn't stop the bleeding. I would say that Sergeant Falco is either lucky or they didn't want him dead. Now excuse me, we need to get him upstairs now.'

Park contemplated what the doctor had said for a moment. If the idea wasn't to kill him, then what was the plan? He called Captain Bridge with the update as he didn't know if Kathy would be out on a call.

***

Kathy walked back in the office after a workout. She had needed to release some stress. She was starting to understand why Will did it so often. The captain walked across the office to her.

'Sergeant Hill, can I speak to you for a second?' He turned to where Alpha team were sitting. 'You too, Hargreaves.'

225

They went into Kathy's office; Captain Bridge closed the door.

'I just heard from Park about Falco. It's not bad news but it's not the best.'

'What's wrong with him?' Kathy asked as she sat behind her desk.

'He has a serious infection, caused by bits of metal coming away from the bullet and lodging in his arm tissue. He is in the operating theatre now to remove them.'

'That kind of ammo is really rare. Surely we can get a lead on it somehow?'

'Possibly, would be easier if the suspect wasn't in the morgue but that's Falco for you. Park said there have been two others killed by these so we can start there. This isn't our case but we can help, but don't allow this to get outside your teams. We don't want anyone getting hold of this in case it gets out and it stops us catching them.'

'So, will he be OK?'

'I'm sorry, Hill, I don't know; it's a waiting game but Park will keep us informed.'

Captain Bridge left and went back to his office.

'Do you honestly think he will be OK, Tom? It sounds really serious.'

'Of course, I know it sounds bad but straight after shift I will take you to the hospital. OK? Now let's see if we can get hold of those case files for Park; it may help catch them.'

'Is this what Will was like when I was shot?'

'More anger than tears, but he was worried.'

'How did he carry on with work? I mean, he caught the guy while I was in surgery.'

'Because he had to.'

It took just thirty minutes to trace the case numbers for the other victims that had been killed by the man who had shot Will, and the medical examiner's office had an ID on the suspect. Tom put them together and took them to Park's office and left them with his partner, Detective Southern. Tom had no idea where all this information was going to lead and he couldn't think of anyone from Will's past that would do this. He didn't even think that his ex-fiancée could do this, but it had to be personal, and it was someone that knew more about his past than anyone that was in his life now.

As Tom got back to the office, Bravo team were heading out on a call. Kathy and her team had been called to a store robbery; she thought the distraction would be good for her as she waited for news on Will.

***

'Sergeant Hill, we just have one armed suspect inside demanding money. The owner had been hit many times so had a silent alarm fitted and now the guy has no way out.'

'OK, sounds simple enough.'

She walked back over to her team. It was strange being in charge without Will being there, but she had learnt enough from him to do the simple call outs without any issues.

'OK, just one suspect. So, Ford you come in with me. Walker, you have the door. Blain and Webb, you have the street.'

The team moved into their positions. Kathy wasn't so tall and this was definitely an advantage when trying to avoid being spotted by a suspect. They got to the door and Kathy looked inside; she could see the suspect and signalled to Ford when to enter.

'NYPD, put your weapon down,' she announced.

The suspect turned around and almost laughed when he saw her; her small height and frame was always underestimated, but leading a team, this was going to be a reaction she needed to get used to.

'You need to put your weapon down.'

'Really, and what are you going to do if I don't?'

'I will have no choice but to fire.'

He laughed, and looked at her shaking his head.

'I'm not scared of you; I mean, I didn't know they made tiny police officers like you.'

'OK, I don't have time to be waiting round all day.'

She fired one shot into his shoulder and he dropped to the floor shouting in pain. Kathy walked over and removed his weapon.

'Not so smug now, are you?' she said to him. 'Control, this is Bravo team. We are all clear here, require EMTs and PD for the suspect.'

'Received, Bravo team, they are on their way in now.'

Kathy and her team headed back to the truck; they were met by a sergeant from the local precinct.

'Thanks, Sergeant, you did a good job. I hear your guys haven't been qualified long.'

'No, Sergeant, they passed on Monday.'

'And I have to say you have a better attitude than Sergeant Falco too, which is nice.'

'I'm sorry?'

'It's a good thing, Sergeant, believe me; I have worked with that guy on so many calls and he has a bad habit of shooting them in the head or just giving me lots of grief.'

'Well, maybe you deserve it, Sergeant.'

'Look, I'm just saying…'

'I know what you are saying. Do you even realise how tough it is to work on SWAT? We are the ones that get sent in when all you lot are too bloody scared to get shot at. We work exceptionally hard to be the best, the elite of the force, and you think it's OK to talk shit about the best officer in our unit just because he does his job.'

'Listen, sweetheart, I don't mean any harm.'

'Call me sweetheart again, Sergeant, and I will have your badge after I put a bullet in your ass.'

Kathy walked off; Ford stood there trying not to laugh.

'You do realise she is engaged to Sergeant Falco, right?'

***

When Kathy got back to the office, she got a coffee and then she heard the captain shout.

'Sergeant Hill, get in here!'

Tom looked at her curiously as she walked across the office. She went in and shut the door and then stood opposite the captain who sat behind his desk.

'Sergeant Hill, I have to say I'm a bit disappointed with the phone call I just got. I was extremely surprised to hear that you had a go at the sergeant in charge at the scene. Sergeant Falco seems to be rubbing off on you a bit too much.'

'I'm sorry, Captain, he made some comment about Falco and I lost it.'

'Really, what kind of comment?'

'That he tended to shoot suspects in the head and gave him a lot of grief, and then he thought it appropriate to call me sweetheart.'

'Well the grief bit I can definitely believe of Falco, but the rest was a little out of line. However, Sergeant Hill, you can't go reacting at call outs like that. I have enough to deal with when Falco gets the PD wound up.'

'Yes, Captain.'

'I am prepared to let this one slide due to the circumstances with Falco, but I don't want to be shouting you in here every other day. I like the way you work, Sergeant, don't change.'

'Yes, Captain, have we heard from Park yet?'

'Not yet, but as soon as I do, I will let you know.'

Kathy left and walked back over to her office. Tom appeared at her door and went in, closing the door behind him.

'What was that about? Last call not go well?'

'It went fine till some sergeant went mouthing off about Will and I sort of had a go at him.'

'You had a go at someone?'

'Do I come across as a soft touch or something?'

'Hell no, I have seen you in action but it's just more Will's style to start falling out with the PD, that's all.'

Kathy went and sat down behind her desk.

'Well, someone has to keep the PD on their toes while he's off, and you, Tom, are just not up to that,' she laughed.

'Hey, I can lose my cool, I just don't need to when Will is around. He definitely does it enough for everyone.'

'Do you reckon all this could be because he pissed off the wrong person?'

'That would be a long list, but Park seems to think it's someone who knows him really well.'

'Definitely not anyone on the force then. I just hope we get them and get Will back as soon as possible.'

'Yeah, me too, but won't be long now till we can go and see how he is.'

Chapter 24

Detective Park sat by Will's bed. Will had been in in the operating room for just over an hour. It had taken a while to get the pieces of metal out as they were very thin and fragile. All had gone well though and he was on strong antibiotics to help fight the infection. Now they were just waiting for him to wake up. He had been in the room for forty-five minutes and was still asleep. It was a private room and Park had sat there the whole time, and Fremont was still outside the door. Just then Will moved and opened his eyes.

'Shit, why does it feel like I've been hit by a bus or something?'

'Sergeant Falco, welcome back.'

'What the hell happened?' Will asked, looking around trying to work out where he was.

'You collapsed at work, scared the hell out of a lot of people. You are in the hospital. Just let me tell the doctor you are awake.'

Park left and a few moments later, a doctor came in to find Will trying to disconnect the tubes and wires.

'Sergeant Falco, what are you doing? Please leave those alone. You need them to ensure you don't end up back in here in a few days.'

Will stopped and looked at the doctor.

'OK, what's wrong with me?'

'You have a serious infection originating at your gunshot wound from yesterday's incident. The bullet was a special and very rare one; it shed metal as it hit your arm. It embedded into your arm tissue. We had to take you to the operating room to remove the pieces; there was five in all. If the infection hadn't been treated when it did, it could have killed you.'

'So, what now, I presume the infection will go?'

'Yes, if you leave that line in your arm and let the antibiotics do their job, and you need to rest, no stress at all. You will need to stay in tonight and most likely tomorrow so we can keep an eye on you.'

'OK, I can do that, I guess.'

'If you want to get better, Sergeant, you don't have much of a choice. I will check on you in about an hour.'

The doctor left. Will sat looking out of the window, reflecting on the last couple of days and everything that had happened; it was a lot to take in. Park came back in and sat down. Will turned around and looked at him.

'Can you call Kathy?'

'I just did, told her you were awake and doing OK.'

'Thanks.'

'Can I ask you something, Sergeant?'

'Stuck here in this bed, do I have a choice?'

'In my office a lot of the detectives said you were difficult and no one knows anything about you,

234

personally I mean, and here I am, new to the city, and you have let me into your life, no questions.'

'Yeah, I don't let people into my life. When people know I have money they change, so I learnt to keep people at a distance, but then I fell in love with Kathy, and she has recently showed me that it's OK to trust people with certain things. She said if I didn't let you in and trust you just a little, we may never find out who was doing this, because you couldn't do your job and someone who watches my back no question is trusted.'

'Well, I appreciate that trust, Sergeant, and believe me you can trust me; Kathy is right, it makes it a bit easier to catch someone when the person they are after co-operates. I am just going to go and make a call, be back in a minute.'

'Yeah OK, can you ask if I'm allowed a drink, I could murder a coffee.'

'Sure thing.'

Park left and Will turned back to the window. He could see the blue sky and the surrounding buildings. He was lost in his thoughts when he heard the door close. He turned around, standing there was his ex-fiancée.

'Carla, what the hell are you doing here?'

'Well, I phoned the department to say thanks for yesterday and they told me you were here.'

'You could have left a message.'

'I wanted to see how you are.'

'Why? You haven't bothered in years.'

'After I saw you yesterday, I realised I still have feelings for you.'

"Really and what feelings are those, because it's clear to me it was never love.'

'How can you say that? We were amazing together.'

'Until I refused to give you what you really wanted.'

'You really think I just wanted your money?'

'Yeah I do, and you married a millionaire, so I figure I was right.'

'I don't love him, it's only ever been you, Will. I didn't want your money; I just wanted you to trust that I didn't.'

'You actually expect me to believe that?'

'I can look after you. After all this I think you should retire from the force. Then we can have kids, as many as you want.'

'Wow, you've got some nerve.'

'Will, come on, you know it makes sense. I am the best match for you and you know it.'

'Do I? Carla, I haven't seen or heard from you in years, not that I'm really that bothered.'

'Not bothered, that's not what people told me. You can say that all those women were for fun but we both know they were all because you couldn't get over me.'

'That was not to get over you, Carla, I told you that yesterday, and now I have Kathy and I am extremely happy, so you can go back to your husband.'

'You will never be as happy with her as you were with me.'

'I already am, she understands me.'

'And likes your bank balance no doubt. I mean, she isn't from money so probably loves the park views, and the expensive gifts.'

'She didn't even know when we got together, so no.'

'Really? Oh yes, I forgot you are embarrassed about having money and hide it from your police friends.'

'No, I just don't trust people because most end up being like you.'

'Will, me and you make sense, both from the same circles. This woman has no idea what our world is like; she will never fit in and will never understand our world and you know it. So have your fun, I can wait for you while my divorce goes through then we can be back together.'

Kathy and Tom walked in just in time to hear her last comment.

'Carla, what a not so nice surprise,' Tom said as he walked past her.

'Oh, how nice, you are still doing your poor friend outreach programme.'

'Excuse me?' Tom replied.

'And who's this?' Carla asked, gesturing towards Kathy.

'This is Kathy my fiancée.'

'Seriously, her? Will, darling, you have been scraping the bottom of the pile.'

'I'm sorry, who the hell are you?' Kathy shouted angrily.

'Sweetheart, I'm the woman Will should and will be with.'

'Carla, that's enough!' Will shouted. 'I don't want or need you. I love Kathy and Tom is a better person than you will ever be, so I think it's time you left.'

Just then an alarm went off on one of Will's machines. A nurse came running in.

'OK, all of you out,' she said. 'Go on out now.' She ushered all three of them out and came back to check Will.

'The doctor said you need to rest, no stress.'

'Yeah, I know, but no one gave my ex that message.'

'Well, we will keep her out, and there will be no more visitors not even your friends.'

'Oh, come on, it wasn't them.'

'I don't care, these machines tell me your blood pressure and heart rate and when they go up the alarms go off, which is what just happened. You need to rest and avoid stress for a good reason. You were extremely ill when you came in here and we need to ensure that you recover not get worse.'

'Can Kathy come in at least? She is my fiancée.'

'OK, she can come back in, but that's all at least for today. I will be telling the officer at your door the same and all the staff.'

'OK, can she come in now?'

'Yeah, I will let her back in, if you promise no more stress.'

'I promise.'

The nurse left and Kathy came back in.

'Are you OK?'

'Yeah, I think so.'

'What was all that about?'

'Well, that was my ex-fiancée, Carla. I saved her life yesterday, so today she decided she wanted me back, and because of the little outburst you are now the only one besides Park and my guard that are allowed near me.'

'Really, that's messed up.'

'I know, right, but I am on strict orders by the doctors to rest. They are monitoring my heart rate and blood pressure and that's what the alarm was, but I'm glad they let you stay and that you are here. Can you stay a while?'

'Yes, of course, I can stay all night just let me speak to Tom and let him know what's going on with the visiting.'

'I'm not going anywhere.'

Kathy came back after about twenty minutes and sat down next to Will. She brought a cup of coffee in.

'Park asked me to bring you this. He has gone back to the office and said I can call if I need to. The captain is sending someone from nights over to take over from Fremont so he can go home too.'

'Can't you be my bodyguard while you are here?'

'No, I'm off duty, it's been a weird day.'

'Why, what happened?'

'Nothing I can't handle, weird not having you there though.'

'Well, I will be back soon enough, and perhaps it's better this way, find your feet better, without me interfering.'

Kathy laughed and took his hand; she was so relieved he was going to be all right.

Chapter 25

Friday morning Will was released from the hospital. He was still in a lot of pain but the infection had gone so he was feeling a lot better and back to his usual self. Detective Park collected him, as Kathy was at work and he was still assigned security detail by Captain Bridge, which he was finding annoying but there wasn't much he could do about it today. Will got in the car.

'Going straight home?'

'No, I want to go to the office first.'

'Thought you were on leave and committed to resting.'

'I am, I just wanted to see the guys and speak to the captain, half an hour max.'

'OK, but no longer. Because you need to get home and rest.'

'Right, and I don't need you or anyone else constantly reminding me of that.'

'I have been entrusted with your care, so it's on me if you don't.'

"No, you are looking out for a stalker, so why don't you just stick to that?'

Park recognised that Falco's confidence was coming back, that he had heard so much about and had experienced when they first met. He wasn't sure if that was going to be helpful in him resting. They arrived at the office fifteen minutes later. Will went straight upstairs to the office, Park followed.

'Hey, guys, how's it going?' Will asked as he walked in.

'Hi, Sergeant, are you back?' Harvey asked.

'No, not yet but soon.'

Tom walked over to him.

'Coffee?' Will nodded. 'Didn't think you was back till next week?'

'I'm not, just popped in to say hi and I wanted to speak to the captain.'

Just then Kathy appeared at her office door.

'Thought you were going home,' she said sternly.

'So, I can't stop by now?'

She gestured to him to follow her into her office. He went in and she shut the door behind them. Will sat on the edge of her desk. She stood arms folded in front of him. He pulled her closer but her pose didn't change.

'You're mad at me.'

'Yes, you were supposed to be going home to rest.'

'So everyone keeps telling me.'

'Will, this is not a joke, you collapsed and just spent the last two days in hospital. I didn't try coming in for weeks after I had been shot and you would never have let me.'

'I know, Kathy, I came to see the captain, and I thought it might reassure the team to see that I'm OK, after my ex made the doctors stop any visitors.'

'OK, that's a fair point. I'm just worried, that's all.'

'Don't worry, I heard the doctors; I am going to take it easy, I promise.'

'All right then.' She relaxed and moved towards him. 'So what do you want to do later?'

'We are having dinner with your parents.'

'Shit, I forgot about that. We could cancel if you don't feel up to it.'

'Your parents already caught their flight, so not really and I am fine.'

'But the doctor said no stress.'

'I'm sure it won't be that bad. I mean, you haven't seen them since you moved. It could go really well.'

'Probably not, but if you need to leave at any time you only have to say.'

'OK I will, now come here.' He pulled her as close as he could and kissed her. He hadn't been properly alone with her in days; it quickly turned more passionate. Will suddenly stopped.

'Let's save that for later. I need to go and see the captain and you are getting me all excited.'

'OK, but later because I have missed you a lot.'

Will stood up. He paused and took a deep breath before kissing Kathy on her head.

'I love you, and don't be too late home tonight.'

'I will try and I love you too.'

With that, Will left. Park sat talking with the team. He grabbed his coffee Tom had made him and walked across to the captain's office. He knocked and opened the door.

'Sergeant Falco, how are you?'

'Not bad considering,' he said as he walked in. He closed the door and sat down.

'So, when I can expect you back?'

'I'm not sure, all this has made me wonder if I should come back at all.'

'Now those are words I was not expecting. What's brought this on?'

'This whole week: someone is trying to get to me and is willing to use people I care about to do that. They had me shot, and that infection could have killed me.'

'Falco, you are an amazing SWAT officer and you have dealt with a hell of a lot, including worse than this, but not once have you ever wanted to quit, because it's not who you are. You have SWAT running through you; it's part of who you are and I know that if you stop now you will regret it.'

'Maybe it is me after all this, maybe it's all a bit too much this time. I have been doing this job so long that maybe it has stopped me seeing what effect it has been having on me and my life. In all my years I have never been that close to dying and believe me, it's a wakeup call. I know every time I go out on a call I can get shot but this was different.'

'OK, Falco, here is what I am thinking. Firstly, don't rush this decision. Second, talk to Kathy about it and third, come back next week and we can discuss it again then. I don't want to lose you because that would be the worst possible outcome, and if you do this, the person responsible wins.'

'OK, but I have had two days to think about nothing else.'

'But that was in hospital recovering. It isn't a time or place to make these kinds of decisions.'

***

When Will had got home he had fallen asleep and woke up really late. He had wanted to give himself plenty of time to get ready but it hadn't happened. So, when Kathy got home, he was pacing up and down frustrated and only half dressed.

'Thank God you are home.'

'What's wrong?'

'OK, you are not allowed to laugh, but I can't get my shirt or jacket on.'

Kathy tried her best not to laugh.

'OK, let me grab a quick shower then I will help you.'

'Good, that's good, but don't take long because we can't be late.'

After about fifteen minutes, Kathy got out of the shower and walked into the bedroom in just a towel.

Will was sitting on the bed with his clothes laid out next to him. She walked over to him and was about to pick up his shirt when he pulled her close to him.

'Maybe we can be a little bit late,' he said mischievously.'

'Later, you have to impress tonight, remember.'

'Yeah, but that was before you came in here with just a towel on.'

'Will, we need to get ready, and besides it will give you something to look forward to during dinner.'

Kathy helped Will with his shirt and jacket, but couldn't get his tie right as it was not something she had ever needed to learn. He put on his shoes and checked he had everything, then picked up the tie.

'You get ready and I will go downstairs and get Charles to help me. We don't have long though.'

'No worries, give me fifteen minutes.'

Will went downstairs. He leaned against the side of the elevator as it went down. He was actually quite nervous about tonight. He couldn't remember the last time he had met a girlfriend's parents and been judged as to whether he was good enough but he was willing to put a brave face on and his usual charm for Kathy's sake. He knew there was a good chance they wouldn't like him as he knew how much they had loved her ex-fiancé but he was hoping to make them see he was a better fit for her. Charles was sitting at his desk as always watching the small television that Will had put in for them.

'Charles, I need your help. Can you do my tie? Kathy can't seem to get it right.'

'Yes, of course, arm still bad?'

'Yeah, it is, but don't let on to Kathy. I am meeting her parents tonight for the first time and she is worried enough about it. Doctors said it is healing but damn it hurts. I don't remember it hurting so much when I was shot last time.'

'Maybe it's because of where it is, I mean, you use your right arm a lot especially that part of the muscle.'

'That's true. I am just hating not being able to do the most basic stuff; it's driving me crazy.'

'There, all done,' Charles said as he finished.

'Excellent.' Will looked in the mirror in the lobby. 'It's perfect, thanks.'

Just then the elevator door opened and Kathy stepped out. She was wearing a stunning red knee-length cocktail dress that hugged her figure. Will smiled at her.

'You look sensational.'

'Thank you, so where are we going?'

'The Plaza, it's where your parents are staying.'

'You booked them in the Plaza, seriously? They will be loving that, I'm sure.'

'I hope so. I got some work to do tonight so I thought I would charm them a bit.'

'I'm sure it will work. You managed to charm me.'

Kathy took his arm and they walked across the lobby to the door.

'See you later, Charles, and thanks again.'

'Anytime, enjoy your evening.'

The hotel wasn't far from Will's building so they walked arm in arm, enjoying the warm summer evening. They didn't talk, just walked slowly, enjoying the moment. When they arrived, they went into the lobby. Kathy had never been inside before and she was amazed by the size and expensive décor throughout. She looked around as they walked through towards the front desk. Kathy suddenly froze. She let go of Will, turned around and started walking back towards the door. Will followed, confused, and stopped her.

'What's wrong?'

'I can't believe it; my mom has brought Tony.'

Chapter 26

'Tony as in your ex-fiancé Tony?'

'The very same. I'm sorry I had no idea she was going to bring him with her.'

Will stood for a moment; then he took a deep breath and looked at her.

'I'm just guessing here, but you haven't told her about me, have you?'

'I told my dad. I talk to him all the time, but he obviously hasn't told her and I just don't speak to her that much.'

'So that's a no then?'

'Will, you know it's not that simple, but you can go if you want to, I understand.'

'And leave you to tackle this on your own, no way, and nothing speaks louder about having a new man than me being here.'

'But no stress, remember.'

'I'm not stressed, I'm fine so let's go and do this, together.'

Kathy composed herself, took his hand and they walked to where her family were waiting.

'Kathy darling, you look lovely,' her dad, Frank, said as he leaned forward and hugged her.

'Thanks, Dad'

'Kathleen, you look nice.'

'Hi, Mom, thanks.'

'Wow, Kathy, you look stunning,' Tony stated. He was six foot and had blond hair. He was muscular and had an arrogant persona. He was wearing a cheap suit and Kathy, looking at him now, wondered what she had ever seen in him.

'Thanks, Tony, Mom didn't say you were coming.'

'No, I wanted to surprise you, and who is this?' Debbie asked.

'This is Will.'

'Good to meet you, Will,' Frank said and shook Will's hand.

'You too.'

'Kathleen, could you accompany me to the ladies, please?'

'Yeah, sure.'

Kathy followed her mother across the lobby and into the ladies. She had a feeling that she knew what was coming. Her mother stood at the mirror adjusting her hair and applying lipstick. Kathy leaned against the counter top.

'What do you want, Mom?'

'I don't know what you mean.'

'Yes, you do, you brought Tony for a start and then you ask me to come in here with you.'

'I was hoping to make you see sense, young lady, go home with Tony where you belong.'

'Wow, not one of you have been to see me since I moved here, and you think I will just drop everything and go back to Chicago.'

'Yes, I do, it's what's best for you and you know it.'

'No, actually I don't, and I have no intention of leaving New York.'

'Well, maybe Tony could be persuaded to move here then. I will talk to him.'

'Don't bother, Mom,' Kathy snapped.

'Why not? Tony is a wonderful man and he has never lost his feelings for you.'

'Did you just ignore the fact that I am with someone and he is out there right now?'

'Sweetheart, you can't be serious.'

'I am very serious.'

'Well, it must be embarrassing for him with Tony coming here for you.'

'No, but you should be embarrassed.'

With that Kathy left and went back to find Will. She found Tony standing with her dad; they were very quiet.

'Where's Will?'

'He went to check to see if the table is ready.'

'OK.'

Just then her mum came back over.

'You need to consider your future, Kathleen.'

'I'm not doing this now, Mom.'

Will walked back over. He could see something was going on and looked at Kathy knowingly. She tried to smile back.

'Our table is ready.'

'You guys, go through. I want a couple of minutes with my girl.'

Will took Debbie and Tony through to the dining room. Frank and Kathy followed a little slower.

'So that's Will, he seems very nice.'

'He is, Dad, but I can't believe Mom brought Tony.'

'I tried my best to talk her out of it. I knew you wanted us to meet Will, but she wouldn't listen, as always.'

'It's fine, Dad, don't worry. I know what she is like sometimes, but I could maybe use your help to get through dinner. I have a feeling this is going to be an attack on my job again so I go back with Tony.'

'Anything for my angel.'

They caught up with the others at the table, which was in a quieter corner of the restaurant. Will always got the best tables wherever he went to eat. Her mom had made sure that Tony was next to her, but Will was too, and her dad was between Will and her mother. Will stood as she approached. He met her with a kiss on the cheek and guided her to her seat. She noticed her dad smile with approval. They sat in relative silence as they chose their meals and ordered. Tony picked up the wine and offered some to Kathy.

'No thanks, I have work in the morning.'

He then poured some for Debbie and himself. Will had made sure that there was orange juice on the table for him and Kathy. The silence was killing Kathy so she decided to start a conversation with her dad to start them off.

'So, Dad, how's the room?'

'They put us in a suite, can you believe it?' he exclaimed like an excited child. 'It has two bedrooms and the shower is bigger than our whole bathroom at home, and I swear you could do laps in the bathtub.'

'Glad you like it.'

'You must have saved for years to pay for this,' her mom added. 'Tony had to take the spare room in the suite. I mean, who can afford one here on a firefighter's pay. I mean, he's doing well now with the promotion but still.'

'I didn't pay for it, Mom.'

'Well, I hope you don't think we can afford it; we have plenty but these prices are excessive.'

'No, Mom, Will paid for it.'

Tony nearly choked on his drink, and Debbie looked astonished.

'Oh, I see.' She looked at Will. 'You must have a really good job, Will.'

'Actually, I work with Kathy.'

'Really? You mean you left the force; well, I am glad to hear that.'

'No, she didn't leave, I mean, I work on SWAT.'

Her mom's face suddenly changed; she appeared almost angry.

'I see, so it's you that encourages her,' she sniped.

'You must be pretty high up then,' Tony chipped in, 'to pay for this,' a hint of jealousy in his voice.

'No, I'm a Sergeant. I run Alpha team.'

Tony and Debbie looked at each other somewhat confused. They knew a sergeant wouldn't be on that much money. Frank decided to step in and help.

'Really, Will, that sounds interesting. What's Alpha team?'

'The teams are phonetic. Alpha team is the sniper team and basically the best, Dad. I was on that when I moved here till a few months ago.'

'Yeah, Kathy, was one of the best I've had on my team too.'

The food started to arrive and the conversation stopped for a while as they started to eat. Kathy was stressed and Will could sense it; he placed his hand on hers and held it for a moment to reassure her. She looked up and smiled at him. She was really glad that he was there.

'So, Kathy, why did you leave Alpha team if you are that good?' Tony asked.

'Because she now has her own, Bravo team,' Will said proudly. 'They work alongside Alpha team.'

'Right, but it can't be that demanding though, just showing up and shooting people,' Tony said with sarcasm in his voice.

Will and Kathy looked at each other then looked at Tony, who carried on eating, waiting for an answer.

'SWAT are the best trained unit on the force, both physically and mentally,' Will answered.

'But it's not like being a firefighter though.'

'No, I carry guns not hoses.'

Kathy tried not to giggle. Tony looked angry.

'Right, because you kill and I save lives.'

'Will saves thousands of lives every year as do I,' Kathy said angrily.

'Not in burning buildings, or up numerous flights of stairs though, right.'

'Wow, arrogant much,' Kathy snapped. Will put his hand on hers again.

'No, Tony, I do it usually with bullets flying at me, and in Manhattan we run up a lot of stairs; the elevators are often switched off especially in hostage situations. The other week we had a call on the twenty-fourth floor of an office block and we had to get up there fast, so yeah, it can be tough and we still need to be able to aim straight when we get up there, but you know, I have a lot of respect for firefighters. I know a few, good guys they are.'

Tony went quiet, and they continued eating in silence but as they were finishing it started again. Tony noticed Will was struggling with his right arm.

'What's wrong with your arm? Did you pull a muscle or something?'

'No, I was shot a few days ago.'

'But didn't you say you were the best?'

'Just a hazard of the job, nothing serious, and only the third time in fifteen years.'

'You've been on SWAT fifteen years,' Frank said, trying to change the subject.

'Yeah, eight in charge of Alpha.'

'But you've been shot three times.'

'Yeah, but one was in the vest.'

'Such a dangerous job,' her mom said.

'Not really, for the amount of calls we take, it's a very low figure,' Will said. 'Works out at less than one percent.'

'So, have all your team been shot?'

'What kind of a question is that, Tony?' Kathy asked.

'A valid one, Kathleen. Tony and I want to know if you insist on this career path that you will be safe.'

'So, Will have they all been shot?' Tony pushed.

'Tom has had two in the vest, Stanson is new so no, Bennett and Palmer no. Harvey took one in the shoulder last year, and Kathy just the once.'

'What?' Debbie exclaimed.

Kathy looked at Will and shook her head. He realised what he'd said.

'You were shot?' her mom questioned. 'When? Where? How?'

'A few months back now.'

'And you didn't tell us?'

'There never seemed the right time.'

'It seems there wasn't a right time to tell us a lot of things,' she said, glaring at Will.

'Look, I knew you would over react about it and I'm fine.'

'That settles it, you are coming home with us.'

Kathy stood up. Will stood and looked at her.

'I need some air.' Will was going to follow. 'It's OK, you finish.' She walked off. Will sat back down feeling awkward.

'I just can't believe this. She needs to come home with us now, this has gone far enough, Tony. I know you will take care of my daughter properly and not have her going into danger every day.'

Will was about to say something but Frank beat him to it.

'Will you just stop it, both of you!' he shouted.

'Excuse me?' Debbie said, quite shocked.

'You two sitting there, being rude and judgemental. You wonder why our daughter doesn't tell you anything. I knew she was injured; we spoke every day when she was off work, and she told me all about Will here. To say this is all on him, you two should be ashamed of yourselves by how you have spoken to him. This is the happiest I have seen my angel in a long time. I for one am proud of her promotion and that she has her own team. When I see her with Will, I know she is in love, and that makes me burst with pride and love. She will not be going back with Tony or us, and I also spotted a very beautiful rock on her chain too.' Frank turned to

Will and his tone changed. 'Will, you make my angel so happy, and I look forward to having you as my son-in-law. Now, shall we go to the bar for a drink and get to know each other better?'

'Yeah sure,' Will answered, smiling.

'You two can go back up to the room if you like, I will be up later.'

'Wait, you and Kathy are engaged?'

'Yes, Tony we are,' Will answered as he stood.

Tony and Debbie sat quietly as Will and Frank walked away and went into the bar area. Then they got up and left the restaurant. They saw Kathy coming back.

'You're engaged?'

Kathy didn't answer.

'Your father just announced it in the middle of the restaurant. We will talk about this tomorrow, Kathleen, because, believe me, this is not finished. We are going up to the room. Your dad and Will are at the bar.'

Before Kathy could respond, they were gone. She walked through to the bar area. She spotted Will and went over to him.

'What did I miss? Where's Dad?'

'He went to the rest room. I like your dad, now I see where you get it from.'

'Get what from?'

'Your no-bullshit attitude.'

'You lost me.'

'He just had a go at them in the restaurant about how they had behaved at dinner towards us. They were going on and I was about to say something and he beat me to it. Was a bit disappointed I didn't get to give Tony a piece of my mind, that is for sure.'

'Seriously? He's never done anything like that before. I have never heard him even raise his voice at my mom, and I am sure you will have your chance another day to say something to Tony.'

She smiled and stood next to Will. He wrapped his arms around her. She was beginning to think it could just work out, inviting them.

Chapter 27

The next morning Kathy's alarm went off early but the bed next to her was empty. She got up and went out into the living room where she found Will sitting on the sofa with a coffee in his hand.

'Hey,' she leaned over the back of the sofa and kissed him, 'how long have you been up for?'

'Couple of hours, couldn't sleep.'

'Arm hurting?'

'A bit, yeah, couldn't get comfortable.'

'Well, you can have a rest today.'

'I actually told your dad I would show him New York.'

'What really?'

'Yeah, and don't tell me I need to rest either. It's an easy day compared to going into work and I will only get bored sitting here.'

'Have you called Park to tell him?'

'No.'

'You know if you leave here you are meant to tell him, even if you just are taking my dad out.'

'OK, I will call him. Go get ready, I will make you some coffee.'

***

Kathy walked into the office. Tom was already there but none of the teams had arrived yet. She got a coffee and sat on the end of his desk.

'Good morning, how's Will?'

'Fine I think, but being a pain in the ass.'

'First time you've known him not to be able to work, right?' Tom laughed.

'Yeah.'

'He's always like that when he doesn't work, drives everyone crazy. We are all pretty glad he doesn't get sick often. Just ask Harvey what he's like.'

'So, what do I do?'

'Just let him do his thing. Don't tell him to rest or anything and don't ask him how he is and he may not be quite as annoying.'

'But the hospital said he has to rest, no stress.'

'I know, they did last time he was shot too, but Will deals with things his own way, and if you try and stop him, he will drive you crazy, pretty much like every other area in his life. He stayed at mine last time he was shot and off work, drove Lynne crazy in just two days. We made the mistake of making him rest and believe me it just doesn't work for him.'

'You could have warned me, Tom,' she laughed.

'Where's the fun in that?' he laughed. 'So, anyway, how did it go with your parents? I believe last night was the big introductions.'

'My dad likes Will. They are going around the city today together. My mum brought my ex-fiancé, in an attempt to try and get me to go back with him, and because I don't want to, they just had a go at me and Will all through dinner.'

'Seriously, wow, that's messed up. Glad my family aren't like that.'

'Yeah, but Will handled it really well, didn't lose it at all.'

'That's new for him. Your ex is lucky he has a bad arm and wasn't armed.'

'Yeah, it may have been a blessing he got shot in that respect. I think I was angrier than he was.'

'Yeah, he is definitely rubbing off on you, first getting called into the captain's office.'

'Very funny, Tom.'

Just then Detective Park walked in.

'What are you doing here?' Kathy asked.

'I came to see Stanson. Is he in yet?'

'Not yet, but did Will not call you?'

'No, why would he? He's at home, right?'

'No, he is going out with my dad today.'

'When?'

'Not sure, soon though.'

'Damn it, tell Stanson to call me, OK?'

'Yeah, sure.'

'I will just go and see the captain. Then I will sort out Sergeant Falco.'

***

Will had walked down to the Plaza to meet Kathy's dad. He went inside and saw him standing with her mom and Tony. As he approached Frank walked towards him.

'Are they coming?'

'No, sadly they aren't, Will, sorry.'

'Don't worry about it, we can have some fun. So, what do you want to do?'

'I just want to see New York and why Kathy loves it so much here.'

They stepped outside into the sunshine. It was a warm day. There were lots of people around; the park opposite was busy. Just then Will heard gun shots coming from the park. He ran over the road to see what was happening. He took out his cell phone and dialled 911.

'This is off-duty SWAT officer Sergeant Falco. we have shots fired in Central Park near the Plaza hotel, need assistance and SWAT.'

He hung up and turned to find Frank right beside him.

'What's going on?'

Will was watching the suspect from a safe distance; he knew he couldn't get involved, especially with his arm as it was.

'Guy with a gun, he is talking to a woman with a child.'

'Oh, so what now?'

'We wait for officers to respond and SWAT.'

'Will Kathy come?'

'Maybe, depends if she is already out.'

**

Kathy was in her office going through some training plans for her team when she got a call on her radio.

'Bravo team, we have a report of shots fired at Central Park, reported by off-duty officer Sergeant Falco.'

'Show Alpha and Bravo responding, Control.' Kathy walked out of her office. 'Come on, Tom, you guys are coming too.'

'What? Why? They didn't call us.'

'Because Will just called in shots fired in the park, and if I go without back up, I just might arrest him too.'

Tom grabbed his stuff as did the teams.

'You do know he is probably carrying, right?'

'Seriously, I will kill him if he goes anywhere near this.'

**

At the park Will was leaning on a squad car as the teams arrived. He had already briefed the officers that were first there. He and Frank were chatting and laughing with a coffee in hand. The police had secured the area but were reluctant to go near with a child in the middle of the situation. When the truck pulled up, Will nudged Frank. He beamed with pride as he saw her get out and organise her team. She followed Tom to where the suspect was. Frank watched the whole thing from a safe distance.

'NYPD, put your weapon down,' Tom announced.

The suspect turned but continued to aim at the woman.

'She took my son from me; I'm not even allowed to see him.'

'This isn't going to make that any better,' Kathy stated. 'You need to lower your weapon and maybe you will get to see him again.'

'Maybe!' he shouted. 'I want my son with me every day, but she took him away.'

'Listen, if you fire, or you don't lower your weapon, we will have to fire and then your son will have no father at all.'

The man stood for a moment without moving. He looked at Kathy then Tom and he could see the others too. He took a deep breath and then slowly lowered his weapon.

'I just wanted my son back,' he said, handing his gun to Kathy.

The PD took him into custody, and Tom patted Kathy on the shoulder.

'Well done, you handled that perfectly.'

As Kathy walked back to the truck, she took off her helmet. She went to her dad first.

'Hey, Dad.'

'Hey, sweetheart, that was amazing, well done. I couldn't be prouder.'

'Thanks, that means a lot, maybe you could tell Mom that it's not as bad as what she thinks.'

He kissed her on the cheek and nodded smiling. Will was about to speak, but she cut him off.

'Don't even bother, Will, I am furious with you.'

With that she got back in the truck and they drove off. Tom walked over to Will and he introduced him to Frank.

'Tom, this is Frank, Kathy's dad. Frank, this is Tom, my number two and my very best and oldest friend.'

'Nice to meet you, Tom. What do they feed you all here? Everyone is so tall, not like me and Kathy.'

Will and Tom laughed. It was true though, most of Alpha team were tall except Bennett, and Kathy was one of the shortest on SWAT.

'Can we grab a lift to the office? I wanted to show Frank around, let him get a look at where Kathy spends most of her time. We were going to walk but seeing as you are here, I thought we won't have to.'

'Yeah, sure, come in the car with me. The rest can go back in the other, just have to hope we don't get another call on route.'

They went back to the office in silence, Will trying to work out what he had done and Frank was looking out of the window all the way. They pulled into the garage.

'Tom, can you give Frank here a tour while I pop upstairs?'

'Yeah, sure, need to smooth things over?'

'Yeah, how did you know?'

'I saw Kathy leave and it looked brutal.'

'I have no idea what I did this time.'

'Then go and find out. We will be fine.'

Will went upstairs. Kathy was in her office and he could see Park in with the captain. He walked into Kathy's office and shut the door.

'I'm still mad with you,' she said, without looking up

'Do you want to tell me why?'

'You really don't know?' she replied, slamming her pen down on the desk.

'Look, I know, I shouldn't have been there this morning, but I heard the shots and reacted, and I did wait for the PD to show up. I didn't get involved I just called it in.'

Kathy looked at him.

'I'm not mad at you because you did what you are trained to do; any officer would have done that.'

'Then you really have lost me.'

'I'm mad because you didn't call Park to tell him you were going out when you said that you would. Imagine my surprise this morning when he walked in here thinking you were spending the day at home.'

'Oh, that.'

'Yes, that. Will, you are like a child sometimes.'

'I don't need a babysitter, Kathy. I am more than capable of taking care of myself; I have been doing a damn good job for the last twenty years.'

'He is your protective detail for a reason.'

'Even with a bad arm I can out shoot that guy.'

'You don't get it, do you? I can't lose you. You see this as some sort of game but it's not, it's serious. You were shot and I thought you were beginning to understand. I care too much about you for anything to happen.'

Will sat on the edge of her desk and sighed. Then he smiled at her.

'I guess I'm just not used to anyone actually caring that much about me, I'm sorry.'

'OK, you're forgiven.' She put her arms round him. She felt something behind him. 'Tom was right.'

'About what?'

'You are carrying.'

'Yeah, I always do, I am allowed, you know.'

'I know, but just make sure it doesn't get you into trouble. To be fair I am surprised you didn't shoot someone this morning.'

'Really, why does everyone think I'm some psycho when I have a weapon on me?'

'No, we don't think that, we just know how lethal you can be,' she laughed. 'Now will you go and speak to Park? He needs to know what you are doing today.'

'OK.'

He left her office and walked over to the captain's office; he knocked and went in.

'Sergeant Falco, just the man, shut the door.'

Will shut the door and sat down next to Park.

'I'm glad you are here. I was about to call and come and speak to you. We may know who your stalker is,' Park stated.

Chapter 28

Will was a little surprised. They hadn't had any leads to speak of that he knew about, but he was impressed how quick Park had worked on this.

'Well, who is it?'

'Richards.'

'What? How is it Richards?'

'We found evidence that she gave instructions to the man who shot you, and we spoke to a contact of Mr X, and he confirmed that someone has been following you, that he saw with Richards on more than one occasion, and he also mentioned he had been given information from another source that confirmed things too. Though he wouldn't tell us who, he did say they were close enough to you.'

Will sat there for a moment letting this information sink in, but he was struggling to believe it. Richards was not exactly the brightest officer he had ever met and she had managed to do all this without anyone catching on. He was also considering how Mr X knew all this; he had a contact that was in his life, and that's how he had been tipped off. But why was Mr X still having him watched and why tip him off? It didn't make sense.

'You spoke to Mr X?'

'No, he wouldn't speak to me but we checked visitor records and call records and found him. He was a PI hired to follow you, Sergeant.'

'What the hell for?'

'Apparently, just to keep an eye on you, which we have put a stop to but there is a chance he will get someone else, though not in the short-term. He has had his privileges revoked for now.'

'That's the least of my worries. He didn't want anything happening to me because he warned me.'

'That might be so he can get to you later.'

'How, he pleaded guilty? And has a very long sentence, he won't get out.'

'Well, we will still be looking into that later.'

Will sat back in the chair and looked at Park. He was starting to know he did the right thing in trusting him.

'So, are you going to arrest Richards?'

'No, we don't have enough. Only Stanson saw her dump the phone and there were no prints on it, and the PI won't testify.'

'So, what do we do now?'

'Give her what she wants. You.'

'How do you mean?'

'Well, the doctor said that you were either lucky or they didn't want you dead. She needed you out of the field. The captain said she isn't very good, so she couldn't take you on fully fit. She knew she wouldn't be able to win that one. She couldn't get close to you outside of work either and she didn't even try, which would suggest she knows you somehow, so this was her only option.'

'But what does she want and why? I have no recollection of meeting her and I have never been to Denver, ever.'

'That's the part we don't know; we can't figure out why she targeted you? It is possible that she worked out you have money though we aren't sure how as your records are pretty much sealed, except for the most senior officers on the force. There is no criminal record or anything. She has one brother and they lived in Denver for most of their lives since she was about six. We can't find a connection to you at all. We know there is more to it than just you dropping her from Alpha; she made it her aim to get here to this unit and your team.'

'So, what do I do?'

'Come to work next week. We will monitor her phones to make sure she hasn't got anything else planned, and we wait for her to make a move. You will have a mic on you at all times.'

'What do you mean anything else planned?' Will was worried.

'To keep your team out of the way, to do what she wants to do. After all, they are nearly as good as you.'

'You think she would harm them?'

'At this point I think she is capable of anything to get to you.'

Will stood up and walked to the filing cabinets. He leant against one with his arms straight and looked down. He took a deep breath. This was like some surreal episode in a television series and he was mad with himself for not seeing it. He, Kathy and Tom had known something was off with her, but never imagined anything like this.

'OK, I'll do it.'

'Good, we are going to brief Alpha and Bravo teams before Richards gets in for her shift.'

'She is working today? And the teams will know it's her?' he said, turning to face Park.

'Yeah, but we aren't ready so it will have to be Monday, and if she isn't prepared, she won't do anything today anyway.'

'Then you best keep her away because after Kathy and Alpha know it's her, they are going to want her ass.'

'We know, Stanson and Bennett already know and we had to stop them retaliating before we have more on her. Delta will be going out on training today; we have an on-call team coming in.'

'Let me tell Kathy.'

'Yeah, we can do that. I will go and get her.'

Captain Bridge went and got Kathy from her office. When she entered, Park left and let him speak to her alone.

'What's going on?'

Will was sitting on the edge of the captain's desk and he looked up at her.

'It's Richards.'

'What is?'

'The stalker, the one who had me shot.'

'You're kidding me. She did all this.'

'Yeah, she did, but they don't have enough to arrest her.'

'OK, then let me in a room with her.'

Will stood up and moved towards her and took her hands.

'As tempting as that is, they want to use me as bait to get her.'

'What, no!'

He looked at her and sighed.

'You already agreed.'

'Yeah,' he nodded.

'When is this going to happen?'

'Monday, I just need to come into work and wait for her to make a move.'

'Monday, you aren't ready to come back. You haven't even had your stitches out yet.'

'That's the point. They don't think she will come after me if I'm fully fit and back on full duty, and she could do much worse to me next time if she doesn't get what she wants from me.'

'Which is what?'

'They don't know.'

'So, what do they know?'

'They know it's her. I need to do this, Kathy.'

'I know.' She stepped closer and put her arms round him, laying her head on his chest, his wrapped his arms around her. 'As long as they keep you safe or I will have something to say to Park.'

'I bet you will, but I'm sure it will all work out.'

***

When Kathy got home, she found her dad sitting on the sofa with Will, laughing about something; it was nice to see them getting on so well

'Hey, how was the rest of your day?' Will asked, getting up and giving her a kiss.

'Tense after the briefing.'

'Thought it might be.' He wrapped his arms around her.

'You guys look like you had a good day,' said Kathy, looking up at him.

'Yes, we did. It was a great day, and we laughed a lot. What do you want for dinner?'

'I'm not bothered, you two can choose, but after today can we stay in?'

Just then Frank's cell phone rang, it was Debbie. He put it on loud speaker as he answered and put it on a cushion. Will and Kathy moved to the back of the sofa to hear better.

'Hello,' he answered.

'Where are you? You've been gone all day.'

'Yeah, I spent the day with Will. I told you that I would be this morning. We have been out and about but I'm at his place now. Kathy just got home.'

'Oh, I see.'

'Did you want to come and meet us somewhere?'

'Where?'

They gestured to each other in silence.

'Why don't you come here? We are just discussing where to eat.'

'And did you decide?'

'We were thinking of ordering in; Kathy has had a long day.'

'So, we would all eat at Will's place?'

'Yeah, why not? Let's move on from yesterday.'

There was a pause for a moment, but they could hear mumbling between Debbie and Tony.

'OK, where is it?'

Will signalled to Frank.

'Will is going to come and get you. It's not far from the hotel.

'OK.' She hung up.

'Kathy, why don't you go and have a shower while I go and get them?'

'Yeah, OK.'

She went off into the bedroom. Will walked round and sat back on the sofa next to Frank. He paused for a moment but he needed to know.

'They have a problem with me, don't they?' Will said to Frank.

'I won't lie to you, Will. They don't like you and have spent the whole day trying to work out where you got your money from.'

'Really, I don't understand why that's important. I guess you didn't tell them then.'

'What makes you think I know?'

'Because you never questioned it: the hotel, this place, and I know you and Kathy are close.'

'Yeah, I know everything. She told me before you guys got back together when she first found out, and she didn't know what to do. She wanted to be with you but was struggling to deal with the fact that you hadn't told her for so long. But it's not my place to say anything to anyone else, that's up to you, but be very careful what truths you tell because Tony can't be trusted and my wife just can't see that because he always gave her what she wanted with Kathy. Until Kathy joined the force anyway, so she sees you as the one that put a stop to the future they had planned for her, when in fact you are a much better fit than Tony ever was. He wanted to control her and you embrace her for who she is. I'm really glad she found you.'

'I'm glad you think so and thanks for being honest with me. Now I best go and meet them.'

***

Will met them in the lobby of the hotel and he walked them back to his building. They didn't speak at all; they got into the elevator and gave a curious look to each other when they realised it was a private one. When they got to the top, Will opened the door and let them go in front of him.

'Hi, Mom, have you enjoyed your day?' Kathy asked as she met them at the door.

'It was OK, we didn't really go far.'

'We weren't sure what you would want to eat so we waited.'

'Right, well, what's the choice?'

Kathy guided them round to the sofas and handed them a couple of menus to look at. Tony sat looking around before he looked at them. Will went into the kitchen and leaned on the counter, watching them. Kathy followed.

'Are you OK?'

'They don't like me much.'

'What makes you say that?'

'Your dad told me and they didn't speak all the way here.'

'They don't know you.'

'They don't want to. Your dad is great but your mom, that may never be a good relationship.'

Just then her dad walked over.

'We have decided.'

'OK, what do they want? I'll call now,' Will replied.

Kathy walked back over to Debbie and Tony; they were sat talking very quietly.

'Will's ordering the food.'

'That's nice.'

'Nice, he's paying again and it's nice.'

'What do you want, Kathleen?'

'I don't know, for you to make an effort with him.'

'Why, it won't last?'

'I'm sorry.'

'Kathy, your mum and I have been looking at a few things and they don't add up.'

'Really, and what are those?'

'His job doesn't explain all the money he has for a start, that he lives here and can afford the Plaza for us. Do you know if it comes from legal means, or are you just happy when he spends it on you? because I can't see any other reason you would choose him over me.'

'Wow, I really don't know how to answer that.'

'Kathleen, we are concerned about him and the kind of person you are becoming; you have changed since you came here, keeping secrets.'

'Me and Will haven't been together that long.'

'But you have known him since you moved here. He was your team leader and obviously a big influence in you cutting yourself off from us.'

'It was actually him that told me to invite you to New York. He convinced me I should.'

Just then Will and Frank walked over. It was obvious something was going on.

'You will love this, Will; my mom and Tony think you are corrupt or something because of all the money that you have and actually asked if you got it legally.'

'Kathleen!'

'What Mom? He has a right to know what you are thinking and saying about him.'

Will stood next to Kathy, put his arm round her and kissed her on the head. He looked at Debbie and Tony for a moment. He smiled. It wasn't the first time people who didn't know him had jumped to that conclusion.

'You should have just asked me. If you must know and if it will stop all the speculation, I inherited this place when my parents were killed; they were quite wealthy and I am an only child. I don't shout about it because it's my business and certainly not yours.'

There was a silence in the room. Tony and Debbie looked at each other, clearly embarrassed that they had got it all so wrong, though Tony was unsure as to whether to believe it. He was still extremely jealous of Will and he wasn't going to let Kathy go that easily; he just needed to keep Debbie on side. Just then the elevator bell went.

'Food's here, shall we eat it out on the roof terrace?' Will said, walking towards the door.

'That's a great idea. If you all want to come this way.' Kathy showed them down the corridor and out onto the terrace.

Will took the food and plated it up and took it outside. When he had got all the food and drinks sorted, Debbie stood up.

'Will, I want to apologise. I was wrong and my behaviour has been terrible. I should have asked you.

You make my daughter happy and I wish I could have seen that earlier, so maybe we can start again and I can get to know you better.'

Will sat back and looked at her.

'You are right your behaviour has been terrible. I encouraged Kathy to ask you here to try and rebuild your relationship. I don't take too kindly to being disrespected or treated in such a way because of my job, or that I am happy to have Kathy working alongside me. She is a grown woman and will always make her own decisions on me and her job; she doesn't need my permission and she sure as hell doesn't need yours or Tony's. Now, if you are honestly willing to start fresh then fine, but I will defend myself and Kathy from anyone, including you. Now shall we eat?'

The meal and the rest of the evening went well. They chatted about many different things, including work, which was a surprise for Kathy, that her mom took so much interest. Kathy felt so happy and relaxed and it was great for them to finally all be getting along. Tony stayed quiet.

On the Sunday, Kathy and Will spent the whole day with her parents. Tony had been encouraged to get an early flight home. They toured the sights around the city. Will had grown up in New York and knew every inch of it so could take them to unusual places too that he knew they would like, and they had an amazing day. Frank and Debbie said they would have to come out more often to see Kathy, which had made her so happy. Will was distracted though as the day went on, knowing tomorrow was the day, and for once he wasn't looking forward to going to work.

***

On Sunday morning Price woke up. He turned over and Richards was still there next to him from the night before. He hadn't meant to take her home with him but after a few drinks it had seemed like a good idea, and this morning he wasn't even regretting it. His phone went; it was Captain Bridge.

'Morning, Captain, what can I do for you?'

'Price, we have a meeting tomorrow afternoon and I want all team leaders in attendance.'

'OK, Captain, I will be there, I'm on shift anyway.'

'Also, Sergeant Falco will be back in the office, and he wanted to go through some training plans with you.'

'Yes, Captain, no problem.'

'See you tomorrow, Price.'

Richards looked at him.

'What was that about?'

'Just work, I have a meeting tomorrow with all the team leaders.'

'Will Sergeant Falco be in then?'

'Yeah, he's back in from tomorrow. Why do you ask?'

'No reason, just glad he's OK after collapsing, that's all.'

Price got up and got dressed. Maybe it had been a bad idea bringing her home. It looked like she still had that crush on Falco and was settling for him instead. After he left the bedroom, Richards sent a text.

We are on, tomorrow morning he is back in the office.

She laid back on the bed and smiled. She knew sleeping with Price would get her information on when he would be back in. It was going to be just perfect and this time tomorrow she would have everything she deserved and more.

Chapter 29

Monday morning Will was already up as Kathy's alarm went off. He was in the kitchen with a coffee. He already had half of his uniform on.

'Morning, not getting ready at work?'

'No, you know I'm still struggling so I thought this would be easier.'

'OK, you need some help?'

'Yes, please, let me just finish my coffee. There's one here for you too.'

'Are you OK?' she said as she picked up her cup.

'Yeah.'

'Worried about today?'

'Not really, just want to get it over with.'

***

When they got in, Kathy helped Will with his handguns. Will wanted to be prepared in case Richards was armed, and he suspected she probably would be. He went into the captain's office for a quick chat about what was going to happen. He then went into his own office and sat down. Kathy brought him a coffee.

'All set?'

'Yeah, just a waiting game now, I guess, but at least I can catch up a bit on paper work; it stacks up when you aren't here.'

'Sure does.'

Just as the rest of the teams were arriving, Alpha and Bravo got a call out. As they left Will got a text from Park.

'This could be it.'

Will saw Captain Bridge cross the office and go out, which meant he was the only SWAT officer there. He started going through his paperwork and signing off on reports and training that Tom had been in charge of. He drank his coffee and looked at his clock. He wasn't sure how long this would take but he had a feeling it wouldn't be long. About ten minutes later Richards appeared at his door. Will looked up.

'What can I help you with, Richards?'

'Glad you are back, Sergeant.'

'OK, is that all?'

She stepped into his office, and moved forward slightly towards his desk.

'You don't recognise me, do you?'

'Should I?'

'Well I know it's been thirty years but still, I recognised you straight away.'

Thirty years is a long time, Richards, so why don't you just tell me what you want, and who you are.'

'My dad worked for your parents thirty years ago. Then they had him arrested and he killed himself in prison.'

'What?'

'I believe you called him Uncle Ned. I used to come by your place. We would play together, in the park or on the terrace.'

'I remember Uncle Ned vaguely. You're his daughter?'

'Yes, after he died me and my brother were taken to Denver. My mom didn't want to stay here; it had been bad enough through the trial, so much crying and anger.'

'OK, but what does that have to do with me?'

'I've come for what your parents took from us.'

'I don't follow.'

'Well, a few years ago, my mom told me what happened, how dad was blamed for something he hadn't done. I mean, if he stole millions then where did the money go?' She moved closer. 'I then decided to come and talk to your parents, but discovered they were dead so I needed a new plan.'

'Which is?'

'You are going to come with me.' She pulled a gun from behind her. 'And you can put yours on the desk because from here I won't miss.'

Will put both of his guns on the desk. He was so tempted to just shoot her but he didn't because he needed answers as to why. She took his guns and put them in a filing cabinet so he couldn't get them easily.

'Now get up.'

'Where are we going?' he asked as he stood.

'City Hall, we are going to get married.'

'Excuse me?'

'Well, it all would have been so much easier if you had just fallen for me, then I wouldn't have had to get someone to shoot you. It would have been all nice and romantic, but no, and I have so much to offer. I mean, look at me, I'm hot and very sexy and I even tried to be good at the job. I didn't realise it would be so hard once I got those guys at my last precinct to pass me without actually passing. I thought it would be easy. I mean, it was easy to get on your team. It seems no one wants to work with you. I expected it to take a bit longer actually. I hadn't accounted for little miss perfect Kathy though. Splitting you up the first time was so easy. She is so insecure about you two, which I would never be, but you still wouldn't look my way, would you? That's when I had to come up with this plan instead.'

'I love Kathy, nothing can change that.'

'Yeah, well, you will be marrying me. Then you will sign over your whole fortune, and you will also give me an heir.'

'You do realise that the teams will be back soon so you won't get away with this.'

'Actually, they will be held up for a while. That last call, my brother has them and won't let them go till we are married, so let's go.'

She took hold of Will and made him walk in front of her, gun pressed into his back. They were just about at the door when she heard a noise behind her. She turned them around.

'Detective, I should have realised you wouldn't be far away, but we are just leaving.'

'Sorry, Richards, you won't be.'

'I have a gun right in his back. If I fire, he's in a wheelchair.'

'You won't shoot him; you need him to get what you want.'

'Are you sure about that because I already had it done once, and besides, you can't hit me from there.'

Just then she felt a gun at the back of her head.

'Yeah, but I can.' It was Stanson.

'Officer, you need to back off before I put a bullet in his spine.'

Just then in a quick move, Will reached behind him, grabbed the gun, pulled it round the side of him and twisted it so she let go. He moved away and Park arrested her, while Stanson kept his gun on her.

'Well, you just signed the death warrants to Kathy and both the teams, didn't you?'

'Actually, they are downstairs with your brother in custody,' Stanson answered.

'What? This should have worked. I planned it all out.'

'Well, you made two mistakes, Richards. Stanson saw you dump the phone after you had someone shoot

288

Falco, and your brother was seen following Falco by someone who didn't want anything to happen to him.'

'Well, Sergeant, you are finished. I won't stop till the world knows who you are. Everyone will soon want a piece of you and your billions.'

Park took her away before she could say any more. Will sat down holding his arm. He looked at his hand and there was a bit of blood.

'You OK, Sergeant?'

'Think I pulled my stitches grabbing the gun.'

'Do you want a lift to the ER to get it checked?'

'Yeah, if you don't mind.'

Downstairs Kathy saw Richards as she was being put in a squad car. She still couldn't believe she hadn't seen this coming.

'You know you will never be good enough. You come from different worlds. You don't understand money and how it works. He will leave you for someone in that world soon enough.'

Kathy slapped her across the face.

'Sergeant Hill, don't let her get inside your head,' Park said as he got her in the car. He shut the door and turned back to Kathy. 'Sergeant Falco loves you and don't ever doubt that.'

As they drove away, Will came down the stairs with Stanson. Kathy walked over and grabbed hold of him and kissed him. She looked at him and smiled.

'I'm just going to go to the hospital.'

'Why, what's wrong?'

'Nothing, I just pulled my stitches, and it's bleeding a little. I won't be long, OK?'

'OK.' She kissed him again.

He walked over to one of the cars and Stanson got in the driver's side.

'See you soon,' said Will as he got in.

They drove away. Kathy couldn't shift what Richards had said and she started to wonder if it was true.

Chapter 30

Will was at the hospital, sitting with Stanson, waiting for a doctor. They were in a room in the ER. It was busy after an accident so it was taking a while to get seen, but they didn't mind as Will knew he wasn't an urgent case. He was actually quite comfortable, lying on the bed, and Stanson had found a chair to sit on.

'Listen, I just wanted to say thanks, for today and for finding that phone. Without it we might never have known who it was.'

'No worries, Sergeant, I'm Alpha team now so part of that is always having your back, right?'

'Yeah, that's right, but I like to say thanks where its due, especially as we didn't get off to the best start.'

'I completely understand, Sergeant. Kathy is an amazing woman. I would be very protective too.'

'Good, glad we are all OK with that, and about what Richards said.'

'Sergeant, I didn't hear anything and even if I did it will not go any further; it's not my business.'

'OK, thanks.'

'Sergeant, I will be honest. When I applied for SWAT, I was hoping one day I would make it onto Alpha team. It has been my aim since I joined the force, so I won't give you any cause to get rid of me now.'

Will sat up and looked at him. He was quite surprised by it.

'You didn't seem that keen when they put you on Alpha,'

'Yeah, I know, after the thing with Kathy I was jealous of you and didn't like you very much, and the other thing is I wasn't sure that I was ready for such a big step. I didn't want to fail at this.'

'Well, you are ready and you have proved you are good enough, so relax. We can train more when I'm back, get that shot a bit better and we will need to work on the sniper range too, and don't forget to keep up with the fitness training. I know you keep pretty fit anyway but it's vital. Maybe we can work out together and I can give you a few exercises that have worked for me.'

'Sounds good, I am always willing to improve.'

Just then the doctor came in. He took off the dressing and had a good look at Will's arm. He pulled at the skin a bit, which caused a bit of pain but he seemed pretty happy with it.

'OK, these stitches can come out,' he said, taking his gloves off.

'Really, but it was bleeding earlier.'

'Probably because you pulled them a bit. It can happen as the wound heals but it looks pretty good to me, but once they are out, we will clean it and have another look, but it's pretty much healed up.'

The doctor left and a nurse came in and slowly removed the stitches. When she was done, she cleaned it and then went to fetch the doctor.

'Just one question though, Sergeant. Do you think Richards will actually tell everyone about you?'

'I've got no idea, but it will sure as hell make my life harder if she does. I may not be able to carry on with the job.'

'That's ridiculous, can you not deny it or carry on anyway?'

'I don't know, it depends how much backlash there is from it all. The team have been to my place but they don't know what I'm worth except Tom. The rest of the PD could cause issues for me if they wanted to, especially if I have pissed them off at some point, which in many cases is likely.'

'But it would be a shame to let all those years of hard work go to waste. I mean, you are the best at what you do.'

'Yeah, it would be a shame, but the future right now is not in my hands.'

The doctor came back in and checked Will's arm again; he got him to move it around and tested his pain levels.

'OK, I'm pretty happy with that. It has healed really well. I want a dressing on it for a couple of days, but you can go back to work, light duties for a few days. Don't overdo it, build up slowly. I presume you are right-handed, so listen to what your body is telling you and when it gets too much stop. Don't lift any weights either for a couple of weeks. If you let it heal properly it will be stronger in the long run.'

'OK, thanks,' Will said as the doctor left.

'Wow, that's good news, Sergeant, get back out there.'

'Yeah, it is. Shall we go?' Will got off the bed.

'You need it dressed first, Sergeant.'

'Yeah, good point, just can't wait to get back, I guess.'

***

They arrived back at the office and Will headed straight into the captain's office.

'Captain.'

'Falco, how's the arm? Hargreaves said Stanson took you down to the hospital.'

'Yeah, it's fine. In fact, they cleared me to come back, on light duties though for a few days.' He sat down opposite the captain.

'OK, welcome back. You changed your mind about leaving then?'

'Not sure, Captain, I guess it depends if Richards tells everyone who I am.'

'Yes, we were quite surprised when we listened to the recording. I am guessing you didn't remember her.'

Will shook his head.

'No, I guess my parents shielded me from everything that happened; I was just a kid, but I remember her dad vaguely but didn't realise who she was till she said. It must have really eaten away at her to do something like this though.'

'Don't try and find excuses for what she did. Yes, she has been through a lot but what she did was inexcusable.'

'I won't, Captain, and I will make a decision soon; I have a lot to consider.'

'Well, keep me informed.'

'Will do, Captain.'

Will got up and he closed the door as he left. He grabbed a coffee then went over to Kathy's office. The teams were down in the gym training. He knocked and went in, closing the door behind him.

'Hey.'

'Hi, are you OK?'

'Yeah, fine, and the doctor has cleared me to come back, on light duties.'

'Really, so soon.'

'I know, I was shocked. Apparently, I heal fast.' He sat on the edge of her desk.

'That's great, I think.'

'I have to be careful not to injure my arm at first but it should be all good in a couple of weeks.'

'You will be glad to get back to work.'

Will looked down. He hadn't discussed the possibility of leaving with her yet. She looked at him and knew something was wrong.

'You do want to come back, don't you?'

'I'm not sure, and it depends on Richards. If she announces to the world who I am it will be tough, and I was considering what to do in the hospital.'

Kathy got up and walked round to him. He looked at her and smiled.

'You are seriously thinking of giving this up?'

'Yeah.'

'But you love it so much, and you are the best in this whole unit. I can't imagine you not being here, but I will support whatever you want to do.'

'I know, it will be tough if I leave but I haven't decided what to do and can't till I find out about what is going on with Richards. I'm going to go down to the range for a bit though, see how far off this has made me. I also just wanted to say, you were right about Stanson: he's a good one.'

"Really, I told you.' She put her arms around him and kissed him.

'Yeah, you did, I will back up in a while.'

'OK.'

He kissed her on the head and went down to the range. He knew this injury could send his shot a way off his usual but if he started now, he may be able to get back up to standard in the next week or so. He was still there an hour later when Park came in. He watched Will for a moment before he approached.

'How's the arm holding up?'

'Not bad but not great. I can feel it aching if I aim too long, but I will get back to full strength soon enough.'

Will got his target back and looked at it; it wasn't far off his usual standard. Park approached and looked at it.

'This is not great; well, you are still better than me.'

'Really, come on, show me.'

Park took his handgun and aimed down the range; Will could see so many issues straight away.

'No, your stance is all wrong, watch me.'

Will showed him how to stand properly, and then let him copy.

'That's better, you need to be relaxed. If you tense up as you fire, it will be off, and you need a very stable and comfortable stance, now fire.'

Park fired his clip; they retrieved the target and Will looked at it.

'See, that's not too bad, almost good enough for SWAT.'

'Yeah, OK, I think I will leave that to you. Anyway, I came down here because I have some good news for you. Richards made a plea deal; she is pleading guilty and will be getting fifteen years in a mental health facility.'

'That was sorted quick, but fifteen years doesn't sound much.'

'Well, her lawyer knew she wasn't getting away with it, especially with the recording of you two talking, and because that deal was offered her lawyer also knew an insanity or diminished capacity defence wouldn't work, so took the best that was on offer. She could get more if they don't deem her fit enough to return to society. Most importantly, she can't say anything about you, and even if she did, they will put it down to her being crazy.'

'Well, that's good news. It means I don't have to worry about what she says at least. What about the brother?'

'He got eight years. All he did was hold your team and follow you around, not really major crimes but he got done on conspiracy too.'

'He could still talk though, about me, I mean.'

'Thing is I don't think Richards told him everything and he was three when they left New York. It may have also been mentioned that if he starts mouthing off, he would end up with our dear friend Mr X, sharing a cell.'

'Seriously?'

'And he looked terrified at the thought.'

'You know if anyone finds out about that, you could get in serious trouble.'

'I don't think he will be saying a word; it appears he went through with this because of her, not because he is some hardened criminal, and most importantly you can carry on as you are, and keep doing what you do best.'

'Yeah, I can. Thanks for having my back, Park. Hope we get to work together again.'

'In a city like this you can count on it.'